HIBERNIAN BLOOD

BOOKS BY DEAN F. WILSON

THE CHILDREN OF TELM

The Call of Agon
The Road to Rebirth
The Chains of War

THE GREAT IRON WAR

Hopebreaker
Lifemaker
Skyshaker
Landquaker
Worldwaker
Hometaker

THE COILHUNTER CHRONICLES

Coilhunter
Rustkiller
Dustrunner

HIBERNIAN HOLLOWS

Hibernian Blood
Hibernian Charm

INFINITE STARS

Infinite Waste
Infinite Worlds

A HIBERNIAN HOLLOWS NOVEL

HIBERNIAN BLOOD

DEAN F. WILSON

Cover illustration by Imad ud Din

First Edition 2017

ISBN 978-1-909356-19-1

Published by Dioscuri Press
Dublin, Ireland

www.dioscuripress.com
enquiries@dioscuripress.com

"The world is full of magic things,
patiently waiting for our senses to grow sharper."

— W.B. Yeats

In ancient times, the Romans called Ireland *Hibernia*.
Much of the magic and mystery of the Emerald Isle
has been lost over the years, but those with a second
sight can see the secret life, the hidden world, where
the line between myth and reality blurs. If you can see
that, you've entered the Hibernian Hollows. Getting
out is not so easy.

CONTENTS

Chapter

ARRIVAL

*D*ublin. The Irish call it the Fair City, and at times it's easy to see why. At other times, there's a darker feel to the city, an odd sensation in the air, as if there's a secret life beneath. The brochures never mention it. They say the name comes from *Dubh Linn*, meaning Black Pool, and the historians attribute this moniker to a nearby lake. Yet there's another reason they omit: Dublin is a whirlpool of strange and dark activity. James Halmorris didn't know that when he arrived.

The flight was fairly uneventful, but the landing was rough. The Irish skies were stormy, and the turbulence was terrible. James was used to long flights, but there was something about this one that made him nervous. He had never been to Ireland before. It was always on his list. He would get to cross it off now, but it would be far from what he expected.

The plane landed at 5:14 a.m., and the airport was quiet. James recalled getting strange looks as he went through Passport Control. He didn't think he looked odd. A typical American, slightly paler than most thanks to his Irish heritage, and messy, sandy hair. A kind of stylised roughness even. But nothing to warrant staring. Nothing to elicit whispers.

"What's the purpose of your trip?" the police officer asked from behind the glass window. They called them *Gardaí* here, or *Garda* singular—or simply "the guards" in that mish-mash of Irish and English known as Hiberno-English. This one looked bored out of his mind, but he perked up when he saw the name on James' passport. He was an older guy, one of the "old guard" even. In the increasingly secular country, he was one of the few officers wearing a crucifix around his neck.

"Looking for my roots," James said with a smile.

"That your real name? Halmorris?"

"Well, it's on my passport."

The Garda looked at him with grim eyes. He wasn't the sort who took humour well, it seemed. James was just the type to rile people up, and sometimes that was dangerous.

"That your real name?" the Garda repeated more forcefully.

"Yeah. Why?"

"You don't know?"

James raised an eyebrow. "Clearly not."

"That's a cursed name, that."

James smiled. "So my grandmother said." He always enjoyed her stories. She had a lot of them, and liked to work herself into some. It made them seem a little more real—apart from all the monsters in them.

"You should listen to her then. Sounds like a smart woman."

"I thought the age of superstition was over?"

"Superstition?" the Garda asked. "I wish it were that, son."

"I've had this name since I was born. Hasn't done me any harm."

"And what about those around you?" The Garda shoved the passport back under the glass, as if he was afraid to handle it any longer.

James shrugged. "They seem fine to me."

"And you're going to go mess that up now?"

"Eh, sorry?"

"By digging around."

"I'm just looking for my heritage."

"You're digging graves is what you're doing. Yours and all."

"Can I go now?" James asked. He thought it might sound a little rude, but he didn't feel like listening to more of this nonsense. And it might have just been nonsense, but something about it filled him with unease.

A HUNDRED THOUSAND
WELCOMES

They say Ireland is the place of a *Céad Míle Fáilte*, a hundred thousand welcomes, but James didn't feel welcome at all. As friendly as many were, others gave him strange and dirty looks. He'd sit down and they'd glance at him and get up, and sit somewhere else.

Cursed, he thought. *I'm starting to feel like maybe it's true.*

Everything that could go wrong at his arrival did. The bus was initially delayed, and then it broke down completely. There were no replacements available, and he happened to arrive at a kind of twilight time where there were no buses running from Dublin Airport to Tallaght, where his hotel room awaited.

He stood outside at the Arrivals entrance, waiting for a taxi. He'd been told there were usually lots of them there, but tonight there was a shortage.

"Stranger things have happened," one of the patrolling guards said.

James was starting to think that maybe the strangest things were yet to come.

He sat on his suitcase and looked up at the stars, and that gigantic globe of the moon. The news had said it was a supermoon, so it appeared a lot bigger than normal. It brought to mind all the things his grandmother had said about how the moon could control minds, and how a full moon could make the world a little crazy. He wondered if it controlled taxis too.

He got up to stretch his legs, realising that no one was around. For such a busy airport, it was deathly quiet. There was not a soul in sight.

Then a black saloon with tinted windows pulled up slowly, its lights dimmed to the barest minimum. For something so mechanical, its creeping motion brought to James' mind something else, something primal. It halted, like a predator waiting for the pounce. Then James walked a few steps away, and it rolls slowly forward. This, more than anything, set his heart racing and his eyes wide. It was there for someone else, surely, reason told him, but terror told him it was there for him.

Then the headlights of another car shone upon it, and like a predator exposed, it scarpered. Even as it seemed to flee—and James thought it odd to think of a car in that way—it made very little sound. Even then its lights were dim, until it faded into the black of night entirely.

The car to which the headlights belonged pulled up beside James, and he felt just as on edge with this, except for the brilliant yellow chassis, and the smiling woman sitting in the driver's seat. *Lilly!* He had never met her in person, but after seeing her numerous photos on social media, her appearance was unmistakable. A wave of blonde-red hair, thick ruby lips, fair skin, large red-rimmed glasses, and a yellow cardigan over a floral-pattern short-skirt dress. Quirky was the word that always came to mind, and in her yellow mini, with pink interior, it came to mind more than ever.

Even through the glass, he could hear her let out a scream of excitement on seeing him, and she waved both hands at him frantically before opening the door. He scrambled in, casting his suitcase on the back seat, and closed the door almost before he'd pulled his legs inside.

Lilly pounced on him with a firm and friendly hug. He couldn't really hug her back with the way she'd pinned his arms, but he made an effort all the same.

"James!" she said. "How are you? Oh, it's great to finally meet you in person. How was the trip? Did you get much sleep on the plane? Were you waiting long here? Oh, you should've seen the traffic. I know I said I mightn't be able to make it, but I managed to switch shifts at the bar. Did your luggage get through okay? It doesn't look like you brought much. Is the seat okay? You can pull it back a bit if you need more room. Do you want the heat on? Where are you staying anyway?"

She was like that online, a flurry of questions, but it was a little more overwhelming in person. But he was glad to be overwhelmed. It helped him forget the unsettling moments that went before.

He tried to answer her as best he could, and as best he could remember the questions. She drove off slowly, telling him about her day, and what she'd been reading (books on the occult, no less), and how the cat was sick, but she thought he was doing better than before.

As she pulled off, James noticed the black saloon parked further up. He wasn't sure why it stood out so much to him, but he was glad it was behind them now. What he didn't see was that, as soon as they passed, it started to follow.

KILTIPPER ROAD

"I'll leave you here," Lilly told him as she dropped him off at his hotel in Tallaght. "Is this all right? God, the rain is coming down heavy now. Just as well you're not still at the airport. Sorry I can't stay longer, but my shift'll be starting soon. The night shift. It'll ruin my plans for tomorrow, but we all have to make some money. We can do lunch though, right? I'll give you a call if I'm not asleep. Talk soon!"

The weather had shifted as they got close to Tallaght, and it only seemed to be getting worse. That was another thing the brochures never told you about it. Hell, James wondered how they ever got those sunny photos in the first place.

The Dronmal hotel stood facing the stadium of the local soccer (or, as the Irish call it, football) team, the quaintly-titled Shamrock Rovers. James thought Lilly was making that up when she first told him, but it turned out to be true. The stadium looked a little desolate at night, a kind of unlit colosseum, and James was glad to be under the glare of the hotel lamps.

Inside, the clerk stood to attention like a soldier.

It looked like a nice place from the entryway, and some of James' fears washed away at the thought of a nice sleep in some comfy, clean sheets.

"Don't see you down here," the clerk said when James announced his arrival.

"What do you mean? I have to be. I booked this months ago."

The clerk shrugged. "You're not on the list."

"But I booked a room. 14B. A double."

"14B is occupied."

"But I booked it. It should be occupied by me."

"Says here," the clerk said, turning the monitor around, "that the Kavanaghs booked it last night."

"But I booked it in July."

"Not according to the system."

James bit his lip. "Do you have any other rooms?"

"I'm afraid that was the last one. It's a busy season."

"Are you serious?"

The clerk shrugged again.

"I want to see the manager."

"He's away. Won't be back till tomorrow."

"And where will I sleep tonight?"

Another shrug.

"Is there anywhere else around here?"

"Yeah, but they'll be booked up too."

"Dear Lord ..."

"You could try the one up in Kiltipper though," the clerk said hesitantly.

"Kiltipper? Where's that?"

"Up that long road to the right."

"That long, dark road?"

"That's the one."

"And there's a hotel up there?"

"Well ..."

"Well what?"

"It's a bit of a trek."

"But there's one up there?"

"It's kind of at the edge of the mountains." By mountains, James took him to mean hills. He had seen photos of Tallaght sent by Lilly, and the suburb seemed to be surrounded by quite beautiful hills, which the buildings had yet to completely obscure.

"How long will it take?"

"About half an hour up that road, then another twenty to thirty minutes around some of the smaller, more winding roads to get there."

"So an hour?"

"Give or take."

"And you're sure there's no room here?"

"Positive. 14B is taken. Haven't seen them come in tonight, mind you, but ... it's taken."

"Right then."

"Well, good luck."

"Yeah, thanks."

"Maybe you should go back into town."

"I can't. No transport seems to be running."

"Yeah, it's one of those nights, it seems. But still."

"Still what?"

"That hotel up there is ... strange."

"You mean strange like having the room you booked?"

"No. It's ... people don't really go there."

"Well, maybe they'll have a room for me then."

The clerk didn't seem to get the jab, or just didn't seem to care. He had a place to sleep that night, so it didn't affect him. James wished Lilly didn't have to rush off so quick, and he regretted turning down her offer to stay at her place. He insisted he'd be okay, but so far it wasn't working out that way at all.

"Can you book me a taxi?" he asked the clerk. "My phone's gone dead."

"Sorry, the phones are down here too. On account of the storm."

"Jesus."

"Yeah. Looks like it's down for the night too."

"Can I stay in the foyer for a bit?"

"Sorry, we'll be closing the doors in about fifteen minutes. The manager doesn't like having people hanging around."

"Doesn't seem like he likes customers to have their room either."

The clerk gave his customary shrug.

James shook his head and sighed. He hauled his suitcase back outside, back into the lashing rain. The wind was icy, and it blew against him. He couldn't help but think that even the weather didn't want him to go that way. He persevered though, holding the collar of his coat closed, yanking the suitcase behind him.

He passed by a small mound in what looked like a local park, and he thought it looked rather peaceful until he saw a large pentagram burned into the grass. He presumed it was just some prank by rebellious teenagers, but it set him on edge even more.

The road was long and dark, illuminated by

periodic lampposts, which seemed to give barely more light than the gas lamps of old. For such a supposedly modern city, there was a certain "old world" feel to many parts of it, and this was one of them.

Few vehicles passed by that way, and not a single one of them was a taxi. Yet, when about halfway up the seemingly never-ending road, a car pulled up beside him. The rain made it difficult to see clearly, but James saw a dark car, with tinted windows, just like the one at the hotel.

He walked on, increasing his pace, and the car rolled forward to match. He wasn't sure what to do now, whether to run forward or back, to see if he could make it to either hotel. Yet he knew he'd never make it in time.

Then the black window on the passenger side rolled down, and James stopped. The car halted too, and James could barely make out a man veiled in shadow in the driver's seat.

"Horrible night, eh?" the driver said.

James said nothing. His heart continued to thump out its terrible rhythm. He wondered if the driver could hear it.

"Where are you heading?"

"The hotel."

"In Kiltipper?"

"Yeah."

"I'm going that way."

"Are you?"

"Yes. Hop in and I'll give you a lift."

James hesitated. "I'm fine, thanks." He turned and continued on a few steps, battling the breeze. Every step seemed even harder now.

The car creaked forward, until the driver was peering out at him again.

"Seems foolish to walk," he said.

For a moment, James' mind agreed entirely. But the fear brought back his alertness and his scepticism. *Seems madness to get in*, he thought. For whatever reason, it almost seemed like the driver heard.

"Do you even know the way?" he asked.

"I have a general idea. I'll be fine, thanks."

"You should get in."

Something happened then that James could not explain. There was a gap in his memory. He vaguely recalled turning his head to glance at the driver, then catching sight of the man's hypnotic eyes. Then with a blank of his own, he was sitting in the back with his luggage, with no recollection of having got inside.

It took a moment for him to gather his wits. He wasn't sure what to do. He reached for the handle of the door, even while it was still driving, but then the driver locked all the doors with a click.

"It's not safe around here," he said.

James' heart was pounding fast. He gripped the handle of his suitcase to calm himself a little. He tried to tell himself that there was nothing to fear, that this was just some helpful soul getting him out of some bad weather. Yet something else told him that this man was getting him into something worse.

"So what brings you here?" the driver asked. He looked up, as if to stare in the mirror, but there was no mirror there. It was only then that James realised that the side mirrors were missing too.

James didn't feel like telling much, but he knew he had to say something. "Sight-seeing."

"Seeing the sights, eh? There's some sights to see, that's for sure."

"Yeah."

"And just sight-seeing?"

James thought he mustn't have looked much like a sight-seer. Hell, right now he must've looked like a coward.

"Well, I was hoping to find out more about my ancestors."

"Ancestors," the driver said, seeming to enjoy the word. James thought for a moment he heard the driver licking his lips. "Sure, don't we all want to know more about that?" the driver added. "That said, sometimes it's best not to know."

"Well, knowledge is power, right?"

The driver didn't like those words quite as much. "Yes," he said coolly. "Knowledge is power. The right knowledge though." He looked up again, and it almost seemed like he was staring at James through the back of his head. His voice grew dark and grim. "The right knowledge."

HOTEL HORROR

By objective accounts, it didn't take that long to get to the hotel. But by the annals of James' heart, it took a lifetime. He couldn't quite make it out through the tinted windows, but when he stepped outside, he almost wanted to get back in.

Above the door was a dark, weathered sign, which read: *Umbra Montis*.

Everything about the hotel screamed shade. In the dusk, it was a silhouette of sharp edges, of steeples and flying buttresses that made it look more like a converted cathedral. It was facing north, the place of greatest darkness, and the light that might have fallen on its eastern walls was largely blocked by a canopy of dark trees that seemed not only to not have been tended to, but to have been deliberately nurtured to grow wild and thick, and crush any tiny beams of sunlight in their immense and smothering foliage.

It certainly wasn't like any hotel he had seen before. It was more like a Gothic manor, or an old castle. It didn't even look like it had been renovated over the years. The windows were weathered, and the walls were covered in moss and ivy. It wasn't any surprise that this place didn't get many guests. If Ireland was a place of a hundred thousand welcomes, this wasn't one of them.

The driver brought his suitcase in and ushered him up the steps to the foyer, with its old, marble floor leading up to an immense stairway, which led upstairs on both sides. An older gentleman, who introduced himself as Ebed, was there to greet him. He was dressed in rather old-fashioned white tie attire, as if he was serving royalty. His speech and mannerisms suggested he was more of a butler than a desk clerk.

"This way," he said. He didn't take James' suitcase, and the driver seemed to vanish. James hauled it up the stairs after Ebed, thinking there were a bit too many flights to climb. They didn't have lifts a few hundred years ago.

Ebed led him through a series of winding corridors, a bit of a labyrinth, before introducing him to the darkness of his room.

"Where's the light?" James asked, feeling around for the switch.

"The light, sir?"

"Eh, yeah. Like, a bulb or something."

"Why, I think you have rather gotten the wrong impression," Ebed drawled. "This is, one might say, a *themed* hotel. People come here for an experience of a different time. A better time, even. Many find it relaxing, a way to get away from the toils and troubles of life. So, no, there are no bulbs here. You'll find a candle in the corner."

James tried to hide his sigh. He couldn't really complain now, what with everything he'd been through. At this stage, a room was a room, whether it had any light in it or not. But Ebed wasn't wrong about this place having a theme: that theme was darkness.

"So, how do I settle up?" James asked, taking out his wallet. He had to use the light of the oil lamps in the corridor to see the notes. He hadn't quite got used to Euros yet, and it almost seemed like Ebed hadn't got used to them either.

The butler held his hand up. "It's been taken care of."

"Taken care of?"

"A courtesy of one Caoimh."

"Who the hell is that?"

"You mean you don't know your driver?"

"No, not really. He paid for my room?"

"It's been taken care of," Ebed repeated. That wasn't quite an answer, and the phrase unsettled James. It brought to mind the Mafia definition.

"A tip then," James said, offering the butler some money.

Ebed seemed offended. "Not at all, Mr. Halmorris. I don't do this for the money."

He ushered James into the room and started to close the door.

"I trust you have all you need," he added, a little curtly, with a lot less pleasantness than James expected for someone working in the hospitality business. He wondered if he was starting to feel entitled, if his life in the U.S. Had given him too many preconceptions, if maybe this was really what it was like in Ireland. Maybe there were still a hundred thousand welcomes, but the welcomes weren't warm.

The door sealed behind him, leaving him in almost perfect darkness, except for a sliver of light that crawled beneath the door. The room was dank and dark, less like the modern hotel he expected (and he might have had if fate had not consigned him here) and more like an old castle room. Indeed, it even had an ancient fireplace, as tall as he was, with a large enough chimney to cast an icy draught into the room. It was not lit, as James expected any good hotelier would do, and he wondered if this was to kill off the warmth or the light. He summoned the shadows now with a few logs from the nearby log-holder, casting a match into the sacrificial bonfire. He found it odd that he thought of it in those terms. This country was changing him, and he hadn't even been here a day.

Even the windows seemed to offer no aid against the dark. James was not sure if it was the weather or the age, but it appeared as though the panes were coated in some thick residue that hindered the light. The thick curtains were many-layered with what looked like blackout material, a further funeral pall for the vanquished radiance.

He tried not to dwell on the condition of his room, and was too tired to do much about it. He got into bed and tried to forget the troubles of the day, but no matter how exhausted he was, he found it difficult to sleep. The combination of cold, oppressing darkness, and disturbing creaking noises prevented him from drifting off for long. When he did nod off, it was fitful, and his dreams were unpleasant. He dreamt of the smothering night, and when he awoke in a sweat, he found the waking darkness waiting to smother him too.

Then there was a glimmer of light from the hallway outside his door, which crawled under the gap of the door, stretching out the shadows. It was a yellow light, like a candle, and it flickered momentarily.

Then something lunged at the door, and James sat up in fright, clutching the bedsheets as if somehow they would save him. He looked to reason, which told him that maybe some drunken guest had stumbled in the hallway, but reason was no help when whatever was out there, blocking some of the light, started to bash against the door, and then to scrape and scratch, and pant and heave, and breathe the kind of breaths no human could ever make.

James was so overcome by fear that he did not know how to respond, bar to shake and shiver, and sweat profusely, and breathe his own heavy, human breaths.

Then the sound stopped, in answer, it seemed, to someone or something else approaching. The light grew brighter outside, and whatever stood at the door fled from it with a ghoulish growl. Something else stood there now, and James was just as frightened. If this new fiend could scare away the other creature, what could it do to him?

The light suddenly vanished, and he was not sure if the person or beast retreated. For a time, he thought he felt the presence there. For another time, he thought he felt it in his room, though he heard no door open, and could see nothing in the blinding dark. For an awful time, he lay there in silence, praying for daylight, and knowing that even when it broke, it would barely penetrate into his room, and would do little to shine upon the dark horrors in his heart.

The next morning, James was almost afraid to leave his room—and just as afraid to stay in it. He heard muffled shouting in the room next door, where an old couple were staying. It seemed like they were the only other guests at the hotel. The woman was in hysterics, while the man was trying to calm her down. The sounds moved out into the hallway, where James could hear them more clearly.

"But we paid for the week," he told her.

"Harold, I'm not sticking this out for another night!"

"We'll lose our money."

"*You* can stay. I'm not. No. That's it for me!"

She stormed off, and James peeked through his door to see Harold standing in the corridor, flustered. He spotted James and shrugged, as if to say, "Women, huh?" James shrugged back, which he thought might have said, "Yeah, I guess."

"We booked the week," Harold said, seeming to need to explain himself.

"Yeah."

"We'll lose our money."

"Yeah."

Harold turned around, waving his hand dismissively. It seemed he had resigned himself to stay. There was no convincing his wife. For James, he couldn't blame her. If he had anywhere else to go, he would have went, but then money was tight for him too. He'd already paid for two hotels. He couldn't afford a third. And the way his luck was going, it could turn out worse.

The presence of the other guests made him a little more confident, so once he was dressed he headed downstairs, pausing for a moment at reception.

"Was there," he said, pausing, "some kind of animal in here last night?" He felt foolish even to ask it, and wondered if he had dreamed it.

Ebed smiled. "That'd be Midnight."

"Midnight?"

The butler reached down behind the desk and picked up a Yorkshire terrier, plopping him on the counter. He was a tiny, adorable thing, and certainly not what James had pictured in the horrors of the night.

"And he … eh … scratches at doors?"

"Oh, yes. He's a naughty little one, always upsetting the guests." Ebed wagged an admonitory finger at the poor pup, who baulked at the digit.

Guess I must be imagining things, James thought. He always considered himself to be somewhat lacking in imagination, ruling out any potential career as an artist or writer, or any of the fabled professions of Ireland's finest. He wondered if that was why he got on so well with Lilly, that whole "opposites attract" concept which she was so fond of.

"We'll keep him locked up tonight," Ebed said as

he walked away. "Or you, whichever makes you feel safest." He smiled a kind of mocking smile.

James already felt a little like a prisoner there. *Safe* wasn't a word he'd use at all.

WHAT'S IN A NAME?

James spent that morning at the National Library of Ireland on Kildare Street. It took a while to find it, and he was embarrassed to ask for directions (which would reveal his Californian accent). Initially he stumbled into the main building, where they had an exhibition on the poet W.B. Yeats, replete with the magical artefacts he employed in the mysterious Order of the Golden Dawn (something Lilly had mentioned to him before).

Eventually he was directed to the Manuscripts Department, which he found tucked away at the other end of the street. He almost passed it by, only for a rather odd-looking woman standing at the glass door. On spotting him, she immediately retreated inside. When he followed, she was nowhere to be seen.

Inside, he saw another exhibition, considerably smaller, on the Easter Rising and Ireland's battle for Independence. James wondered if it was fortuitous that he arrived in the country almost exactly one hundred years after that momentous occasion. He thought it odd that he even considered such a notion as fortune. Lilly really was rubbing off on him.

He was greeted by a guard at the desk in the corner. A normal guard, not a police officer. He was finding himself starting to confuse the two.

"I'm looking for the Manuscripts Department," James said.

"Upstairs. Do you have a Reader's Ticket?"

"Oh. Yes." James fumbled in his pocket for the ID card he had applied for many weeks before.

"Second floor. Take the lift."

The guard smiled, and James smiled back.

Upstairs, he found himself in a large reader's room, with many desks dotted throughout, and walls full of volumes and newspapers.

"Can I help you?" the lady at the desk asked.

"Yes. I'm supposed to look through some documents on the Halmorris name."

The lady bit her lip. "Halmorris?"

"Yes. I'm looking into my family name."

The bite was fiercer. "Take a seat. It's not quite quarter to. They'll be up in a sec."

James obliged, taking one of the few remaining seats close to the desk, beside an old woman with a dusty tome on Yeats. As soon as he sat down, she glanced at him and stood up, keeping her thumb between the book. She found another seat further away.

Jesus, James thought. *I'm not making friends around here.*

Just as paranoia was kicking in, the lady at the desk plopped a pile of papers before him. He hadn't even noticed them bringing them in on the cart, or the grey-haired and thick-bearded man who now stood behind the desk like a granite statue, staring at him over his gold-rimmed glasses.

"There's more," the lady said. "There's a lot more."

"Yeah," James replied. "I guess this will be a start."

She headed back to her desk, where she whispered to the grim gentleman, and he whispered back. Between their fervent whispers, they looked at James. He caught them looking, and even looked back, and yet neither of them blinked or budged, or looked away in embarrassment.

James tried to focus on the papers before him, and this was hard to do with the watchful hawks, but eventually he was overcome by the details in the manuscripts, the genealogies, the birth certificates. There was tons of material to wade through, going back generations, and though all of it provided useful information, it somehow felt like he was only scraping the surface. He didn't want to think it, but some of the papers even looked a little new, or falsely aged.

He jumped when he felt a hand upon his shoulder, and turned to see the grey-haired gentleman standing there, his bony claw digging into him. There was no one else in the room, and the light had gone. James hadn't quite realised how carried away with the research he had gotten.

"It's closing time."

"Oh."

"Past closing, actually."

"I'm sorry. I must have lost track of time."

"You must have."

"I'll head off now. I can come back tomorrow."

"Halmorris," the man mused, keeping his grip.

"Yes."

"James Halmorris."

"Yes?"

"Maybe you should come back tonight."

A CONSTANT COMPANION

It must have been madness to go back there in the pitch of night, what with all the strange goings-on. James was feeling like maybe he really was going mad a little. Yet, if he didn't get to the root of all this, if he didn't find some answers, he thought he might go mad a lot.

The old gentleman told him to return at 10 p.m., what he quaintly called "the little witching hour," a phrase that unsettled James a lot more than he expected. He wasn't sure if this was just how Irish people were—naturally mysterious. Or if some of them were toying with him. Or if maybe there was something else at work.

James arrived a little early and sat down on the steps outside. The streets were deserted. On a Monday, the city largely closed shop by 6 p.m., and most stragglers were gone by 7. What few people James did see were the homeless, and those who looked like their home might be a graveyard. There were a few of those sorts, gaunt and ghastly, with pallid faces and shrunken sockets for their colourless eyes. James had met Goths in the U.S., and had some rocker friends in his youth, but these ones seemed a lot more dedicated here.

Just as one of these pale folk hobbled down the road towards him, he heard the door open behind him, and out stepped the grey-haired gentleman. He exchanged a glance with the approaching figure, who halted, and then the gentleman beckoned James inside.

"You meet all types here," James said.

"Umm," the gentleman replied, locking the door and slipping the key into his waistcoat pocket. He stared at James for a moment. "All types."

"So, what's this all about?"

"You'll see."

"Are you always this mysterious?"

"Well," the man said, taking his glasses off to give them a wipe, which James thought he did deliberately to add to the effect, "this *is* a mystery."

He led James through the exhibition area, which looked eerie in the dark, and into the lift. He produced another key from his waistcoat, which seemed to have a lot of them, and turned it in a special lock inside the lift, which James had originally taken for decoration. It was a rather old lift, perhaps from the Victorian era, and it was more mechanics than electrics, shaking violently as it moved. It had a cage door which James had only seen in the movies, and it seemed to climb to higher floors than were even numbered on the buttons inside.

"You'll have to forgive me," the gentleman said. "I'm always forgetting to introduce myself." He held out his bony hand, which had a few large gem-encrusted rings. "Ernest Constant."

James shook his hand. Mr. Constant had remarkable strength for his age. He must have been at least eighty. James even wondered if maybe he had been there to see the Easter Rising too.

"James Hal—"

"Well, we know who *you* are," Mr. Constant said.

"Yeah, I'm kind of wondering about that."

"Well, it *is* on your card." He gestured to the Reader's Ticket which hung around his neck, with his photo and name, and the number 1888.

"Oh, y—"

"And you *did* send your details before."

"Right."

"And you did introduce yourself at the desk."

"Yes, I guess—"

"But we *have* been expecting you for some time. I was starting to think you'd never arrive, that maybe I would shuffle off this mortal coil beforehand, so to speak. And yet ... here you are."

"Here I am."

As the lift shuddered to a stop, and they exited into a vast candlelit library that looked as ancient as the old stone forts of the countryside, the question really was: where was *here*?

THE OLD LIBRARY

"This is what we call the Old Library," Mr. Constant explained. "The untouched part of the building. We've renovated the rest, a few times even. But not here. No … not here."

"It looks like it needs it."

"Oh, you can't repair the work here with masons."

"What about Freemasons?" James quipped.

Mr. Constant smiled and waved a finger. "Not even them." He walked ahead, gesturing dramatically as he talked. "You see, this is one of the old bastions of a bygone era, home to knowledge occult and arcane. Few are permitted to know about it, and fewer to visit it."

"So, what makes me the lucky soul?"

"Lucky?" Mr. Constant enquired. "I wouldn't say that."

He continued on, taking up books as he passed shelves, placing them down on others, seeming to be habitually doing a little bit of librarian duty as he mused on the days of old. He seemed a bit of a fruitcake, if you asked James, someone who might have done well hosting the ghost bus tour that James had seen prowling the city, but he wasn't exactly someone James would trust.

"You're here to find answers about your past," Mr. Constant continued. "And you won't find those in the normal archives, because your past is anything but normal."

"They said my name is cursed," James said. "I doubted it, but I'm doubting my doubts lately."

"Nonsense. Your name isn't cursed. It's a very old name, for a very old family, a family with a duty. You are in the line of the blood wardens, an ancient, noble heritage, one with royal blood. Your family abandoned the crown all those generations ago to protect the world."

"Protect it from what?"

"Evil."

"What, like Hitler?"

"No," Mr. Constant said. "It's not the earthly wars that worry us. The fairy tales, the folk tales, the myths and legends … they are not so untrue as many today would have you believe. This world is not as it seems, and it is only one of many worlds. The stories are wrong in the details—sometimes—but not in the spirit of what they say. We are living among the unliving, and when you walk alone in a graveyard at night, others walk with you too."

He should definitely do the ghost bus tours, James mused to himself. Mr. Constant sounded almost convincing, even like he believed the stuff himself. James wondered how much this private tour was going to cost him at the end. He was sure he'd be paying a special rate to be the "Chosen One."

"So, what does a blood warden do?" he asked, indulging the old gentleman. He wasn't sure how well the old con would do if he was led too far off script, but he seemed to have an answer for everything.

"Keep the peace."

"Can't say I'd make a good soldier."

"Well, you're going to have to be."

"Why?"

"There isn't anyone else. The vampire families have forged a tenuous truce that has lasted this past century, a truce formed on their great reverence for tradition, but as soon as something shifts—and it is shifting, mark my words—they will be at each others' throats—and ours."

"The vampires," James said, smiling.

"Yes."

"Right."

"You don't believe me then."

James raised his eyebrows. "Did Lilly put you up to this?"

Mr. Constant glared at him. "No one put me up to anything. I do this for the good of our world."

"Well, it's entertaining, at least."

"This is not a joke, James. For many it is a matter of life and death."

"Or undeath. Is there an unlife?"

"I see I'm wasting my time."

"Well, you're the one who wanted me to come back here."

"Because I thought you were looking for answers."

"I am. It's just … not to those kind of questions."

"But these *are* the answers, whether you like them or not. Tell me, James, what made you come here? Why are you even looking into your ancestry?"

"I don't know. I guess I felt kind of … unfulfilled. I worked in business, in banking. It was the same damn thing every day. I made money, but I was never happy. I guess I got fed up of the suit, and that damn tie, getting tighter around my neck, choking me."

"So you took it off, let down your collar, so to speak."

"Yeah."

"That's all well and good, James, but don't get too relaxed. You're showing your neck now, and around here, that's very dangerous."

THE NIGHT VISITOR

After all the bizarre things Mr. Constant had told him, James felt on edge. But he was stubborn, and he dismissed it all as superstition, as the nonsensical ramblings of someone born in a superstitious age. Maybe Ireland just had that kind of atmosphere that made it seem like maybe magic was real, but James couldn't accept any of it. He even dismissed the fears he had about the hotel, and went back there that very night, also ignoring the fact that he was the only passenger on the bus route in that direction.

The front door of the hotel was open, and there was no one there to guard it. Not that anyone would wander in. Part of James, buried by false courage, didn't want to either. The place seemed empty.

He headed to bed, locking his door. He might have had false courage, but he didn't have enough of it to leave the door open.

His dreams were restless and dark. He dreamed of Mr. Constant and what he told him, and then of ghouls and ghosts, and witches and vampires. He dreamed of his grandmother, and her father, whom he had only seen in photos, and of some kind of war. He dreamed of blood, a lot of blood. Then he dreamed of something scratching at the door.

He awoke, and the sound didn't vanish into the dream. It kept going. It kept scratching.

James sat up, feeling the terror form in little droplets on his skin. In his mind, Mr. Constant told him that it was a monster. But he knew it couldn't be. There were no monsters but men. For all James knew, maybe Mr. Constant was one of them.

To be fearless and brave is no great feat, but to be afraid, and be daring anyway, that is an accomplishment worth noting. James was very afraid, unlike his grandmother in the dream, unlike the people fighting the creatures there too. Yet he challenged himself to face his fears, partly to prove Mr. Constant wrong.

He got up and made tiny advances towards the door.

The scratching continued. It seemed to grow louder. He could hear panting and rumbling, and low growls. No wonder Harold's wife ran out of the place screaming. James felt like following.

But if reason was right, as it should be, then the noises were nothing. They were the creaks of an old building. They were the whistles of the wind. They were someone playing a prank. They were the sounds of the imagination. They were that little dog, and nothing more.

Or maybe they were something else.

Just like the dream, there was a battle in his mind.

There was only one way to be sure. He reached

for the key in the lock, and though his heart thumped "No!", and though the sweat poured down him, and though his mind begged him to stop, he turned it quickly and heard the latch open.

The sound echoed. The scratching stopped.

All that stood between James and whatever was out there was that door, that wooden panel, with no metal bar holding it in place. Just a little nudge of the handle, and there would be no barrier at all.

James breathed heavily. On the other side, that something else breathed heavily in response.

It's just the dog, he told himself, though he knew he didn't sound convincing. That was the trouble about the inner monologue. It was much harder to lie to yourself.

He grabbed the handle of the door, and he felt it give way a little as something else grabbed it on the other side. He caught his breath and froze, and then, in a moment of daring, which went just as fleetingly as it came, he pressed the handle down and pulled the door open.

He closed his eyes involuntarily and braced for some assault. His shoulders rose and his fists were clenched. They say "fight or flight," but all he did was stand there, waiting.

And nothing happened.

He opened his eyes, slowly. It took some time to adjust to the dim light in the corridor. The shadows seemed to convulse to the flickering of the candle flames, and then congregate in one corner as he entered the hallway.

There was nothing there.

Huh was all his mind could muster. It was a satisfied mental sound though, a kind of "told you so" by reason. If there was nothing there, then it couldn't be a monster. It was just his imagination after all.

Yet, for all the satisfaction of that, he had his doubts. Something about that place made it seem like anything was possible, like maybe the gap between reality and imagination was really small.

He stared down one side, where the shadows seemed stronger, and down the other, where even they did not seem to want to go. That way was in the direction of Harold's room. James noticed that the door to it was slightly ajar.

It dawned on him then that maybe all the noises were just the other guest, maybe someone who woke up from a nightmare (as anyone in that unsettling place might), or maybe even someone sleepwalking.

Or maybe Harold had heard the noises too, and came out to investigate.

For all the satisfaction of finding nothing, no monsters beneath the bed, there was more to be found in the agreement and reassurance of others. So James went to the entrance of Harold's room, where there was a literal gap between the door and the frame.

He rapped his knuckles gently on the wood.

No response.

He repeated the gesture, a little harder, and the door pushed in slightly. It almost seemed to open of its own accord.

There were shadows in that room too, but none of them went near the bed, where the light of the bedside candle shone fiercely. Those ivory sheets were covered in blood. Poor Harold wasn't there, but James didn't have to be a detective to figure out that this was all that was left of him. Harold feared he'd lose his money. He should've feared he'd lose his life.

James backed away, stepping out of the room, until he struck the wall on the other side.

Then he heard the panting and the low, rumbling growls from around the end of the corridor, that end where the shadows would not go. He turned his head slowly in that direction, just as something emerged from around the corner.

THE BEAST OF
UMBRA MONTIS

It reached an arm around the corner, at the end of which was a kind of hand, or a kind of claw. Its fingers were buckled, and its nails were long and curved, and black as death. It dug them into the floor, pulling itself forward a little on that mangled, bulbous arm, with its blemished, mismatching skin. Then its head emerged, swollen and deformed, a mangled mess of lumps, with one large fang penetrating through the roof of its flayed upper lip. It was half-man, half-dog, and wholly a nightmare, with none of the best of man or beast. Part of it was covered in hair, part in skin, and other parts were open sores. It seemed in pain, and looking upon it was painful.

It emerged fully, pressed against the ground as if its own body was a terrible weight. Its back was hunched, and its hind legs were bent and broken, so that one caved in upon itself, unmoving, and the other lay limp, dragging behind it, with its own curved toenails tearing through the woodwork.

Its face was so swollen that one eye was permanently shut. But the other was open, wide and manic, with a piercing gaze that spoke to the soul. What it said, no man or woman could utter, but it suggested that what was done to it, it would do to others.

On seeing the creature, James instinctively backed away. Yet even his own steps were slowed, as if that gorgon glare had turned his limbs to stone, and his will to nothing. It took more effort than it should have to move, and no amount of effort could get that evil creature out of his mind.

The beast was slow at first, but as James regained some control of his body, backing away more swiftly, it started to speed up. There was a hunger in its reddened eye, a desire for flesh and bone, and maybe the gnawing of a soul as well.

James ran, turning on the spot, stumbling in place, grasping the wall for support, finding his footing uneven, his pacing slow. He could hear the lash of nail against wood, and the thump of the body behind it as it lifted itself up, only to come crashing down again. He could hear splintering bone, and the cry of anguish and famine of the beast.

The corridor seemed unending. No door gave way to James' fumbling hands. No window illuminated the path ahead. The oil lamps wafted out one by one as James passed, throwing him and the creature into a more oppressing darkness. The shadows fled with him, making terrible gestures of fear and panic on the walls. The floor groaned beneath their feet and claws, and the beast bashed it and tore at it, until the wood splintered like its own breaking bones.

James glanced back, even as he knew he shouldn't, and he was caught again in the mesmerising gaze, feeling suddenly sluggish, until he could see the beast making a leap for him. James fell, and the creature landed upon him, dragging itself up over him, letting itself collapse upon him, so that his bare skin could feel the bristles of its hair and the dappled texture of its hide, and the wet and burning of its drool, and the slicing sting of its claws. Its weight was unbearable, a crushing force that held back any fight James had in him. And then its face, that terrible uneven skull with its rash-covered scalp, came close, until its eye faced directly James' own.

James thought of Harold, and what it must have been like to have been torn apart by this horrible beast, to have his blood splatter the bedsheets and the walls. He wondered when the pain would end, if it would be quick or slow. He questioned if there was an afterlife, and if life there would be any better than here on earth. Yet he even questioned if maybe this was not earth at all, but Hell, and here upon him was his demon accuser. All thoughts of past and present, and what might be, came upon him like a flood, like the spittle of the beast that washed his face.

And then he realised that it was licking his face, that its coarse tongue was tearing across his cheeks, leaving behind a stinging saliva. This was the taste, James told himself, before the bite, before the tearing and slashing, before the devouring, before the digesting.

But time passed, and none of those things came.

It slurped at his face, but did no more. If anything, when the fear of it all faded just a little, when James had partially accepted his fate, finding no strength in him to fight it, the beast seemed like a playful dog, not a hateful hound.

Yet, when the creature clambered off of him, and James felt the feeling return to his arms and legs, he backed away, scurrying across the floor, until he struck something. He glanced up to see a woman standing there in a long, red dress, the colour of Harold's bedsheets.

"So you've met my pet," she said.

James could barely utter a response. The "pet" still scrambled down the corridor towards them, maybe to the woman, probably to him. Maybe it only came to play. But there was a game called life and death.

"Don't you worry about him," she said, without any sense of reassurance.

The worries came more and more, piling on top of each other like the dead.

"You know what they say," she continued, and she smiled, until her own fangs were visible even in the dark. "Beware of the owner."

THE RED COUNCIL

James did not know if it was the panic of it all, or the
glare of the beast, or the vampire's own hypnotic
stare, but he found his consciousness fading. When
he awoke, feeling drugged and groggy, he was glad
that the candles were dim. Yet it was not the light that
attacked him, but the memory of what came before,
and the threat of what was coming.

He flinched, and felt the tight grasp of rope
around his wrists and ankles. This summoned back
the panic of the beast's restricting weight, and his
eyes involuntarily sought out that creature, sitting at
the foot, and slightly to the side, of a large throne,
where the red-dressed woman sat like a queen, her
dress flowing down to the floor, her figure etched into
the shadows, her silhouette sculpted like a statue. She
sat perfectly still, her right hand resting on the beast's
head, and her left held up, poised and delicate, yet
revealing her own chiselled claws. Upon her hand
was a crown of many jewels, and resting by the arm
of her throne was a serpent-headed sceptre.

Beside her sat another, who wore a kind of long

tunic, dark blue in colour, over a well-fitted and somewhat archaic suit, with frills and chains. He was the epitome of what people thought of when it came to the Victorian era, as if, indeed, he had crawled out of a painting from that time. It did not surprise James that he found himself thinking: maybe he had. This man, if he was a man, also wore a crown, though somewhat smaller than his companion, and there was no sceptre in reach for him.

Around the large meeting room were many others of all types, yet all dark and sombre, with dour, pallid faces that best belonged in the grave. All those eyes were upon James in the centre, tied to a chair, which itself was fixed to the floor with bolts, suggesting that he had not been the first to be restrained there.

"Our guest," the woman said, rotating the wrist of her left hand, until it gestured outwardly, as if to take his own. Perhaps it was meant as a symbol of welcome, but since he could not shake it, it seemed more like mocking.

Suddenly the entire room of people—if they were people—stood up, all in unison, a kind of militarism that was off-putting, like the fists of the dead punching through the earth together. Some seemed a little reluctant to stand, but they stood all the same. All but the woman and the man at the front, who stayed seated on their thrones, and the beast at the woman's side, which purred through its blistered lip.

"You look frightened," the kingly figure said, drawing up suddenly from his seat, and seeming to float across the floor, his gown covering his feet. His shoes made no noise, and only the crumpling of his clothing would have alerted anyone to his movement. He came up close to James, bringing his hand to James' face, caressing his cheek gently, though brandishing his own pointed nails much too closely to James' widened eyes.

"Do not fear," he said. His accent was strange, perhaps of Eastern European origin, albeit mingled with a hint of others. He seemed genuinely concerned, even pained, that James was afraid. He sucked a long breath of air through his teeth, through his fangs, and spoke swiftly, "We mean you no harm." Something about him came across convincing, but James was not sure if this was a mere display, or yet another demonstration of those fiends' hypnotic powers.

The man moved around behind him, and James' eyes followed, until the trail of the vampire's gown vanished into the shadows. He could feel something behind him, but it did not feel like a man. He felt the shiver of someone walking upon his grave, yet the thought came to mind that in this room—this tomb—he was walking inside another's.

"We have called a council," the woman said, stealing James' attention once again. Her voice was as seductive as her dress. He found himself staring at her ruby lips, feeling a sense of yearning, and yet wondering if the ruddiness was from lipstick or from blood.

There was a sudden clatter of fabric, and then a sound like the flap of a bat's wings. With this came a flurry of black, and instantly it seemed that the kingly figure was back on his throne, poised again like a painting.

James' heart fluttered on its own, and in it nested its own blackness, the rot of the soul when touched by the undead.

"I am Lorcan," the king said, and it was clear that he was king. The audience bowed, willingly or not. Even the woman at his side tilted her head to him. "Of House Caomhánach," he continued, "or Kavanah, as the English have it." He didn't sound Irish, nor English, nor really from any place James knew. It brought to mind: *What accent do they have in Hell?*

"And I am Ruagruaim," the queen said, and more than ever it was clear that she was queen. The chamber curtsied again, and even her king nodded in acquiescence to her. "Of that same noble house, but you may call me Rua."

What little Irish James knew was enough to tell him that *Rua* meant Red. It was a fitting name for her, with her scarlet smock and crimson lips. Her hair was the black of deepest night, and her eyes were not far off that colour, but her face was paler than even the most sun-shy Irish cheeks.

Her companion took her hand, and they looked to one another fondly, and then back at James with the kind of fondness for a feast.

"What do you want from me?" James asked through his gritted teeth. He realised he was sweating profusely, and that his hands were clenched tight. The muscles of his stomach were tense, and his shoulders were hunched, as if to reflexively guard his neck.

"You come at a time of turmoil in our world," Rua said.

"At the prelude of a great war," Lorcan added,

rolling his tongue, and licking his lips.

"Among vampires, there are many long-held and valued traditions. One of them is this," Rua said, holding up her and her husband's clasped hands, "our sacred and perfect marriage, built upon the line of queens and kings."

Lorcan turned to her and stared into her eyes. He smiled, and she smiled. Then he caressed her hand, before she turned her attention back to James.

"Another is the long line of blood wardens, of whom you are one of the last."

"I'm not anyone," James protested.

"Be careful," Lorcan responded, with that same look of genuine worry. "If you are not a blood warden, then what is there to stop us bleeding you?"

From the corners of his eyes, James saw the assembly of vampires shifting in place, coming forward a little. They moved like spectres, with no bobbing up and down, just a graceful approach. They came on either side, like the walls closing in—if the walls had teeth.

THE FIVE FAMILIES

With a flick of Rua's wrist, a royal gesture, the wall of vampires halted. How terrifying it was for James to think that with another tiny movement, she might authorise them to advance again. The power she had was unstoppable. It was the power of life and death.

"Tradition forbids us from harming a blood warden," Rua revealed, much to the scorn of one or two of the vampires in the shadow-draped crowd.

"Tradition is our guiding force," Lorcan added. "It is our ... light." He shuddered at the word, and James saw others in the audience recoiling. It seemed even the word itself brought a flicker of brightness into the room.

Rua drew up, letting go of Lorcan's hand, and she descended the three steps at the foot of her throne, letting her dress cascade down behind her like a sanguine waterfall. Her hips swung from side to side, dragging the dress one way and then the other, until she stood in the centre of the room before James.

"There are five claims to the vampire thrones of

Ireland," she said. "Only one of those can be true. *We* are that truth."

There was a murmur of dissent in the assembly, silenced by the crack of her wrist, which was like the lash of a whip.

"Some would question that," she acknowledged, casting the evil eye at one or two in the audience. "Some would question us. Tradition requires that when there are such … disagreements … that we bring in a blood warden to settle the dispute. Or at least to delay it."

"But I know nothing about you," James said. "About this world."

"He's no warden!" one of the audience cried. James turned to see a curly-haired man pointing an accusing finger at him.

"Come and have a taste then, John," Rua replied, "if you doubt him."

John retracted that finger, and then the arm. He didn't come to taste. He didn't even make a step forward.

"He is a blood warden," Lorcan said, coming up beside his wife. "There is no doubt. It has been confirmed by Mr. Constant. This is James Halmorris. You all know that name."

There was a flurry of nods, and a mumble of ascent. Rumour swept through the wave of vampires, all separated into their varying factions, all vying for the thrones, but all respecting the long-held traditions—for now.

It was odd to see that there was a look of hate in the eyes of some, and a look of fear in others. Every time they said "blood warden," James felt some of his own fear fade away, and in its place came courage and strength. Where it came from, he did not know, but it was the same kind of courage and strength his father had, and his grandmother before. Maybe it was in his blood.

"Will you accept this then?" Rua asked the crowd. "Will you accept that we have brought a decider among us? We have brought a peace-keeper. Can we then have peace, and let our disputes be put on hold?"

There was some discussion among the various families present. It was clear that they were kin, for they huddled together, eyeing the others suspiciously. Some said little, turning quickly to nod and bow to Rua and Lorcan. Others talked a lot, and loudly, making condemnatory remarks about the couple, and casting doubt on James.

"How much does he know of us?" John asked in time.

"Not much," Rua replied.

"He should know all."

"Would you trust a blood warden with all?"

"Well, you're asking us to trust him with the thrones."

"Then quickly now, say your piece."

John turned to address James. "I represent the Gorman family. We are *An Lucht Siúil*, the Travelling People. No land holds us. No grave restricts us." It seemed he was making a special effort to speak more slowly for James' benefit, and to avoid using the Cant of his people. "At one time we ruled, but because we would not commit to one location, would not sit in but one adorned chair, our claim to the crown of Ireland was ridiculed and dismissed. We were usurped by the settled people."

"You were not, ya liar!" another in the crowd yelled. He was with the O'Connor clan, and James only knew that by the fact that they were carrying banners bearing their family name and crest of arms.

"Speak when it's your turn to speak!" Rua barked back.

"For now," John continued, "we support the Kavanaghs' claim to the thrones."

"That's because you've got none yourself!" the O'Connor spokesman said.

"Speak then, Cathal," Rua said, "since you find it difficult to do otherwise."

Cathal could barely be seen with all the banners and bunting, but his voice could be heard well and clear. "We go back to the last High King of Ireland, before the Normans came. Of all of us, we have the greatest claim. A hundred of my ancestors held the crown of Connacht, but because the Kavanaghs held the crown of Leinster, where our capital is, they get first call as ever! It isn't right. It wasn't right then, and it's not right now. Tradition might be on the side of the Kavanaghs, but history is on our side. There's more royal blood in my left toe than there is in the rest of ya!"

"Perhaps we should have a toe for a king then," Rua said, without a hint of a smile.

There was a snicker amongst the audience, and Cathal faded back into the shield of banners.

Then an older woman rose on the other side,

where a family of clearly noble birth sat quietly, observing, but taking no part in the back-and-forth of the other families. When she rose, Lorcan stood and bowed, and the entire chamber went quiet.

She spoke in a soft, but firm tone. "I am Ioana, and we are House Danesti from Romania," she said. "We support the Kavanaghs' claim. The traditions of our peoples must be upheld."

She sat back down, but even James could tell that her short speech of approval was largely for show. She looked at Lorcan softly, and James wondered if perhaps they were related, if that explained Lorcan's accent, but she eyed Rua coldly, as if she did not wholly approve of their marriage.

"That just leaves the O'Neills," Rua said, "who are, as always, absent from these meetings."

"A disgrace," the woman from House Danesti said. "We had the same problem with House Draculesti in Wallachia."

"I will speak for them then," Rua continued. "They are descended from Niall of the Nine Hostages, and claim links to the High King of Ireland, the Kings of Tara, Ulster, and others. Yet it is there claim to Niall Noígíallach that they say matters most, for they say that the hostages offered to him by nine different families were, in fact, the first vampires of Ireland, offered not as gifts, but as an attempt to end the O'Neill line. They say then that they are the origins of us all, not necessary as living, but as undead. Any historian, of the mundane or magical world, would dispute their claims."

Lorcan rose. "You have heard enough," he said.

"Five families, three of which are in agreement with the Kavanagh claim."

"This isn't a vote," Cathal said.

"Perhaps not, but while it is unwise to fight one army, it is madness to fight three."

Cathal was silenced by that comment. James had little to go on, but instinct told him a lot that the vampire clans would not say: that the O'Neills, if they had been there, would not have been silent at all—that they might have spoken with the tongue of a blade.

WINDOW

The council room cleared, and James was freed from his bonds, though not before being forced to promise that he would not run, and warned that if he did, they would chase him. It took a great deal of effort to pretend that he was strong, that he did not fear them, and he was almost certain that they saw right through it.

"Good night," Rua said, as she sealed him back inside his bedroom. She retreated through the closing door, with the flicker of a smile upon her face.

He heard the clang of the old bolt locking into place, and felt Rua's presence shifting down the hallway. Perhaps she walked, but she made no noise. There was a grace about her and her husband, but James knew that it was a shell that covered an ugly, evil core.

As soon as he felt he was outside her gaze, James let out his long-held breath. It was not a sigh of relief, because there was still no relief to be had. His own shell of false courage crumbled, and he felt himself tremble. As far as he could tell, there was no one else in the hotel but him—well, no one living anyway.

He rushed over to his bed and grabbed his mobile phone from the bedside table. One bar. While this was Dublin, it was the outskirts, the so-called "best of both worlds" of the city and country life. There were two worlds here all right, and he had the worst of both.

He tried to call Lilly, but he couldn't get through. It didn't ring at all for ages, and then when it did, it went straight to voicemail.

Damn it, Lilly, answer!

Then the bars dropped to zero. He was on his own. His life or death was in his hands, and the claws of the vampires.

He looked around the room for some means of escape. There was nothing but the window, and he was three floors up. He opened it and looked outside. It was a long drop. He would be lucky to get away with just broken legs—and with them he wouldn't get away at all.

He sighed. He was trapped. He would have to go along with their plans, even though he was certain he was no "blood warden," that he had no power against these fiends, and that his only contribution to them would be his very blood.

He saw the single bar on his phone come back, and his heart fluttered. He bashed 999 into the keypad, and was thankful that the operator answered immediately.

"P-p-police, please," he stuttered.

There was a momentary dial tone, but just as swiftly he got through to the police.

"What's the emergency?"

"There's been a murder here. I don't know what to do." He thought it best not to tell them about the vampires. He needed the men in blue. He didn't want them to send the men in white coats instead.

"Where are you?" the operator asked.

"I'm at—"

Then the call cut off, and he saw he was down to zero bars again.

No! he cried internally. He might have cried aloud too, were he not fearful that it would attract the attention of the vampires again.

Yet maybe something heard him all the same.

His eyes were drawn to the open window, where he felt a presence approaching.

Then a hand reached up from the outside wall and gripped the window sill with its long, pointed nails. Then the other came, reaching through the opening and grasping the interior wall. Then the head and body came, and Lorcan crawled into the room.

James dropped his phone, and Lorcan swiftly advanced and caught it. He drew up slowly, clutching the device in his bony fingers, with his nails pointing outwards so as not to scratch the screen.

"Be careful," he said, soft and sweet. He handed it back to James. "Best to put that away," he continued. "Out here, the signal … is not great. Besides, in this land you are the stranger. So, pray tell, who would you call?"

"No one," James uttered.

Lorcan smiled. "No one, yes." He circled around James, so that his gown wrapped around James' legs.

If he kept going, it would wrap around his neck like a noose.

"Why are you keeping me here?" James asked.

"To keep you safe."

"I don't *feel* safe."

"*Good*," the vampire said. "It is better to be afraid and be vigilant, than to think yourself protected, and let down your guard." He walked towards the open window, letting his gown unwrap from James' legs and pull along behind him. He gestured to the opening.

"For example," he said. "It is not wise to leave an open window here. You never know what might crawl in." He smiled. There was something very intimidating about his friendliness, as if he never once in his life—or death—had to make an explicit threat.

"I … I can't breathe in here," James said. "I feel suffocated."

"Yes," Lorcan said. "Breathing. Sometimes I forget these things that the living do. For us, air comes in, like it comes into a deep, dark chamber beneath the earth. It does nothing there. It means nothing to us. But for you, it is different. I barely remember those times. So long ago!" He seemed pained to think of it. "Good riddance!"

He pulled the window shut.

"I know this is all very strange to you," he acknowledged. "It shouldn't be, by right, for your own family should have explained these things. They have taken for granted the peace we have now. Like my forgetting the feeling of air inside my lungs, they have forgotten the wars of the past, and thought little to plan for the wars of the future."

"I don't want anything to do with your wars."

"Neither do I, but we don't get that choice. With or without us, they come, like night comes to smother day."

"Like day comes to douse the night," James said defiantly. He didn't know where that defiance came from.

Lorcan smiled. "See. There is some fight in you. You came here to learn about your roots. These are your roots. This is who you are, who you were meant to be."

"Not who I want to be."

Lorcan scoffed. "Do you want to be afraid? Do you want to live a meaningless life? There are millions who live such … boring lives. Once you enter our world, there is no going back. Even if you returned to America, you would start to see the unseen, and hear the unheard. The secret life, the hidden world, is now unlocked. It cannot be sealed again. Like it or not, this is your path now. Here in Ireland, you were reborn, like I was seven hundred years ago!"

Despite James' fears, he knew that everything Lorcan said was true. After seeing what he had seen, he wondered if he could ever get it out of his mind. He wanted to forget. He wanted to go back to his old, boring life, even though it was that boredom—and a sense of calling—that prompted his current expedition.

"It will take time to adjust," Lorcan said. "But for you, time is short. Time is fleeting. Death for you means death. Death for us means life. We cannot turn you, and we are obliged by tradition to not harm you. Yet tradition does not stay all hands. It does not hold back all fangs. We are at the turning point where the blood wardens are needed again, where mortals referee immortals. I despise that it is so, but like you I have no choice!"

"Why do you need me?" James asked. "What power do I have that you don't? I don't understand any of this. How can I stop a war? How can I compel vampires when you have the power to compel and control minds? I am powerless!"

"You only *feel* powerless. Trust not those feelings. You know not what is in your blood. It is the bloodline of royalty that rules the vampire world, but it is a holy bloodline that runs through warden veins. I abhor it with a deep and powerful hatred! Yet here I am, asking your help. Evil, so-called, beseeching good … so-called."

"And what if I don't help?" James asked.

"Then it matters not that you can now see the unseen, for if this dynasty falls, then chaos will erupt here, and all will see it, and hear it, and feel it. This world will go to ruin. Dark as we may be, we hold back darker forces, bent on destruction. For we may be undead, but be believe in order. We work with the living. Some would have it all destroyed. So then, my fearful warden, do not fear us, but fear what would happen without us."

He turned back to the window and gestured to it. "And now, I have a gift for you. It is one that repulses me, but it will be of value to one careless enough to leave open windows here. Let not there be an open window to your soul!"

He raised his hand, and a wooden box rose up into the air and hovered by the window.

"This is a power that is in my blood, and my father's blood, and all the way back beyond memory. For me, it is weak, but I can move things. And perhaps tonight, I can move your mind closer to where it needs to be, to that fighting force."

He pulled his hand towards him, and the box floated into the room. He recoiled at it, as if it contained something of horror. Yet to frighten him, it must have been something good.

"Hang these by your window," he said, as he clambered out. "For you are lucky it was only I who came through tonight!"

INVESTIGATION

James used the contents of the box to line the window—now firmly shut. There were strings of garlic, crosses, amulets, scrolls with Hebrew, Greek, Latin, and Coptic verses, and strange metal discs with engraved designs. Any other time, he would have dismissed these superstitious items, but now he used them with fervour. He placed some of them near the door as well.

Yet still his dreams were disturbed. He dreamed of creatures appearing out of nowhere, of turning around to see nothing, and feeling something behind him again. He woke in a fit of sweat when he felt a piercing in his neck, and found nothing there, and no blood stains on his pillow. There were no indications of anything at the window or door, which gave him reassurance. It seemed that the only invasion was in his mind.

The next morning, he awoke—still tired—to hear a loud banging at the main door downstairs. He got dressed quickly and unlocked his door, only to find it had been sealed from the outside.

Downstairs, Ebed sauntered towards the giant, metal door. He unlocked it, letting it creak slowly open, so that the sound sent a shiver down the spines of the two people present on the other side. They were a woman, short, with a mix of curls and braids, and what seemed like charms knitted into the bangs. She wore a figure-made suit, which made her look authoritative, but she wore other charms on her wrists and neck, which didn't seem to go with that appearance. Her companion was a taller man in a Garda uniform, clean shaven, with a smug smile on his face.

"Hi. My name is Melanie Rosen," the woman said, "and this is my partner Toby Eckhart."

"A pleasure," Ebed said. "I am Ebed Lónan, keeper of the manor."

"Is this the Kavanagh residence?" Melanie asked.

"This is Umbra Montis," Ebed corrected.

"But the Kavanaghs live here, right?"

"They have a dwelling here, yes."

"Can we come in?"

"Do you have a reservation?"

The woman pulled a piece of paper out of her coat and held it up. "It's called a warrant."

Ebed's eyes widened. "I don't follow. What is the problem here?"

"We have reports of disappearances in the area."

"Disappearances? Oh my."

"Oh my indeed," Melanie said, stepping inside.

"I'm afraid the place is rather empty," Ebed explained.

"I'm afraid I'll have to see that for myself."

Eckhart followed, tipping his hat in a sarcastic manner. "Nice place you've got here," he said. "A bit grim though."

"A bit old," Ebed said. "It dates back several centuries. We've tried to … preserve the décor."

"Is that all you're preserving?" Eckhart quipped.

"I don't follow."

"Oh, I bet you follow just fine."

Melanie walked past the empty reception desk, rifling through the records there.

"It's pretty quiet here," Eckhart said. "*Dead*, even."

"It's off-peak season," Ebed explained. He started to fidget with the buttons on his waistcoat.

"Where are the guests?" Melanie enquired.

"It's … off-peak season."

"You have records of guests here. I see some are crossed out."

"They left."

"Funny, that," Eckhart said.

"Harold Osbourne," Melanie said.

"What about him?" Ebed asked. "The Osbournes left a few days ago."

"His wife left. She reported that her husband never returned."

"We overheard them having a … disagreement," Ebed said. "It seems that perhaps Mr. Osbourne did not want to return to his wife."

"Or wasn't allowed to."

"I am afraid I find your insinuations rather unsettling."

"You should," Melanie said. "I find them quite

unsettling too."

She continued through the records.

"Where are the owners?"

"They are … indisposed of at the moment."

"Like Mr. Osbourne?"

"No."

"I guess you've misplaced them as well," Eckhart said.

"They come and go as they please. I am but a lowly servant."

Eckhart came up to him. "Do they come and go a lot at night?"

Melanie proceeded to wander around the bottom floor, opening doors and peeking inside rooms, while Ebed followed much too closely, seeming on edge.

"Is it just you who works here?" Eckhart asked him.

"Mainly."

"There's quite a lot here to dust."

"Yes, indeed. I'm kept busy, without a doubt."

Melanie continued her inspection, shoving against some doors that were jammed, much to the protest of Ebed, who commented about the age of the building and the "sensitivity" of the décor. Melanie ignored him and forced open several more doors.

"I don't know what you're looking for," Ebed protested. "There's no one here."

They heard a sudden banging from upstairs. Melanie launched herself up the steps immediately on hearing it.

"You were saying?" Eckhart said, before following her up, with Ebed racing up behind them.

They were in such a hurry to find the source of the noise that neither detective noticed Ebed twisting one of the etched bannister knobs. There was a creaking in the building, and elsewhere in the hotel a corridor was sealed off, while another one opened.

They charged through the corridors, following the sound, opening bedroom doors to find nothing or no one there—just clean sheets.

In time they came to a wall, from where the muted knocks seemed to emanate.

"It's coming from the walls," Melanie said.

"Mice," Ebed suggested.

"Or men?"

"I find that rather unlikely."

"We can break through," Eckhart said.

"You cannot!" Ebed objected. "This is a protected building."

"We have a warrant."

"You have a warrant to search the place, not to destroy it."

So they searched further, every level, and yet as big as the hotel was, it almost seemed to the detectives like they could only reach certain parts of it. They mentioned this to Ebed, who raised his eyebrows at the notion, and denied fervently that there was a cellar below the building. They didn't find anything, and were forced to abandon the search.

"We'll be back," Melanie said as they left. She glanced up at the windows from outside, and thought she saw something, but it was gone just as quick.

"Of course," Ebed said. "We'll be waiting."

WHILE THE OTHERS REST

Melanie sat in the car with Eckhart outside, slapping her hand down on the dashboard in frustration.

"Is it wise to mess with them?" Eckhart asked her.

"I guess it's like prodding the beast."

"To put it lightly."

"I have to though. I can't let them keep getting away with this."

"Don't they have special protection though?"

"You mean magic?"

"No," Eckhart said. "I mean from higher up. The government. God, even the Gardaí are in on it. Is it wise to even mess with that?"

"Wise? Maybe not. But right?"

"There are a lot of right things that don't get done, or you end up crossing the wrong people."

Melanie sighed. "I hate this."

"Yeah, me too. But we gotta play it safe."

"We're the OIU. We're not supposed to play it safe."

"We've gotta, or we mightn't get to play at all."

They drove off, and just as they were coming onto the main road, Melanie spotted something in the mirror: two black cars pulling up outside the hotel.

"Stop," she told Eckhart. "Looks like they've got guests."

Eckhart slowed to a halt and peered around. "Is that the Kavanaghs? In daylight?"

Melanie pulled out a pair of binoculars from the glove compartment and stared at the cars. It took some time before any of the doors opened, and when they did, it was a strange sight indeed. All the doors opened in almost perfect unison, like a choreographed display by the mob. Two men, tall and bulky, came out of the back of the first car, and they were shrouded in black, with black balaclavas. Even with these, they started to sizzle in the dull sunlight. Other figures got out with veils and umbrellas, including a familiar woman with frazzled, red hair: Dearg, the head of clan O'Neill.

"Christ," Melanie said. "It's the O'Neills. You better step on it before they see us."

Eckhart didn't need to hear that twice. He sped off before anyone could spot them.

"What are they doing there?" he asked.

"I don't know, but whatever it is, they're hoping to do it while the Kavanaghs are asleep."

Ebed heard the chime of the doorbell and sauntered to the door, thinking it was the detectives again, back to prod and probe like they too often did. He had prepared a little tongue-lashing just for the occasion, but when he opened up, his voice was stolen by the sight of Dearg, her red hair affray, flanked by the gigantic Brute Brothers, and surrounded by many others of the O'Neill family.

Dearg pushed in, and Ebed stumbled back, holding out his hands. If only he had a cross in them, it might have helped a little. But it would not have been enough.

"Y-y-you can't c-come in here," he said.

Dearg scoffed. "We were invited to the Red Council. We're just a little … late."

"The masters are retired. You have to come back later."

"No," Dearg said. "We're not looking for them."

Ebed's eyes widened. He turned a little to shout, "Run, James!" but Dearg leapt at him, tearing his throat apart with her teeth. He gasped and gurgled, and though it was his hope that one day he would taste blood, he never thought it would be his own. Dearg let his body clatter off the marble floor, where he continued to spasm.

"Rip this place apart," she ordered her companions. They split apart in all directions, some heading upstairs, others scouring the bottom floor.

Dearg crouched down to Ebed and patted his head. "I'll be back for this," she said. He only hoped he would be dead before she claimed her trophy.

She headed upstairs, following the echoes of Ebed's shout as she began the hunt for James. Her motto was "strike when the iron is hot," but in this case it meant "strike while the warden is weak—and while his watchers are sleeping."

James heard the commotion from downstairs, and Ebed's fearful shout. He grabbed the handle of the door, but it was still locked. This room wasn't just his prison now—it would be his final resting place. His name was on the computer in the foyer, pinpointing his exact location in the sprawling mansion. He had to get out at all costs.

He kicked the door, but it would not budge. Then he bashed it with his shoulder, but it held strong. He struck it again, frightfully aware of all the noise he was making, and of the pain starting to shoot up through his arm.

He backed away and looked at the window, with all its talismans and adornments. He considered for a moment that he might have to jump out and risk whatever fate gravity had in store for him. Maybe dying like that would be better. Yet something told him that he wasn't allowed to die now, that he still had a mission to accomplish. He'd have to survive the O'Neill family first.

Suddenly he heard heavy footsteps in the corridor outside. These were not like the beast of Umbra Montis, but harder and heavier, like the footfalls of a giant. Then he heard the feet strike doors, kicking them in one by one along the route, until the wood didn't just creak, but screamed.

James hurriedly pulled down some of the garlands of garlic and strings of talismans, but he had wrapped many of them up well to keep them in place throughout the night. He never thought that he would have to fear the day as well. He yanked at them, but only some of them came loose.

Then he heard the boots outside. He could feel the awful presence. Then the hail of splinters came, and Joe O'Neill, one of the so-called Brute Brothers, busted his way inside. He was a colossus, hunching over to avoid the caress of the ceiling, his muscles bulging, his face gnarled. He had a kind of dumb look in his eyes, but it wasn't his eyes you had to fight.

James, surprising himself, made the first blow by casting some of the protective items at the vampire. Joe snarled and backed away, taking part of the wall with him. He stumbled over the ruins of the door, falling onto his back, which gave James just long enough to leap through the cracks and dash down the corridor.

Joe was slow on his feet, and slow to get up, but as James slid around the nearest corner, he found Joe's twin brother, Paddy O'Neill, bounding down towards him. James skidded in place and charged down the other way, turning sharply at intersections, while Paddy crashed into the walls instead.

There was a long stretch ahead, long enough for Paddy to regain some speed as he charged after him. Yet there, on the far end, sat the beast of Umbra Montis, rearing up its horrible, mutilated face. James was already in full sprint, and there were no more turns between these two opposing fiends. The beast reared up and started towards him, dragging itself at first, but then trotting, now running. James gulped at the thought of the impending crash, of both creatures crushing him between their bodies, then landing down on him to finish the job with weight or fang.

Then the beast ahead leapt up, and though one

of its legs was limp, its other one propelled it up to a great height. James slid beneath it, falling onto his side and skidding down the corridor, while the beast snarled and spat, reaching out its twisted claws to Paddy O'Neill. It sliced and tore, and as James got up, he realised that it hadn't leapt for him—it leapt to save him.

But he wasn't safe yet.

HIDE AND SEEK

James fled down to the next level, unsure if he would find more vampires there. He wasn't entirely sure where he was going, but it was becoming increasingly certain that he could not outrun these vampires. He had to hide.

Umbra Montis was a manor with few mirrors, but he found himself in a part of the castle with a small reflective surface nailed to the wall. He wasn't entirely sure it was a mirror, for it seemed more like a silver panel, etched with some strange writing, and what looked like crude depictions of wolves. Yet he could see his own reflection in it, and nothing else.

He peered out into the corridor, drawing back suddenly in fright as he saw the back of a vampire there, who was crawling up a pillar leading to the next level. He decided to make a dash for it while he could, and sneaked out into the hallway, with his own mirrored self shaking just as much as he was.

He dashed around the next corner just in time, for he felt the formidable, palpable gaze of the vampire as it turned its head to look at the path he had just crossed. It cast no reflection, and continued to scurry up the stone plinth.

James had now reached a part of the castle he knew he had not seen before, for things darkened considerably, and he was more reliant than ever on the burning torches that lined the walls, held to the brick by obsidian hands. He couldn't remove one to bring with him, which meant he was forced to enter the pitch of darkness for long stretches before he found the next torch. That was probably a good thing, as the light might attract his hunters.

His toes suddenly felt a precipice, and he drew back just in time to see that he had reached a winding stairwell, which led down deep beneath the earth. There were fewer torches here, and likely the vampires did not need them.

He began the slow descent, clutching the brickwork for support. The fear of what was above propelled him down, but the fear of what was below slowed his steps.

In time, he emerged in a vast catacomb, an underground network of passages and tombs. It was damp and musty, and the air was hard to come by. The vampires didn't need that either.

He crept through, hoping to find Rua or Lorcan, whom he had been scared of only a day before, and hoping he didn't find something else. It seemed that many of the tombs were empty, while others were filled only with bones. James wasn't sure if these were deceased vampires or their victims.

Despite searching many passages, he could find no sign of his hosts. He began to worry that maybe he had found some abandoned area that wasn't used by the Kavanaghs, not a refuge but a dead end.

He started to hear sounds from upstairs, and the light flickered by the end of the stairwell. The hunters had brought the hunt to this level too.

James frantically searched about for somewhere to hide. There were nooks to hide in, where the shadows might disguise him from human sight, but he had a feeling—a dark and horrible feeling—that the vampires would see him there with ease.

He half-ran, half-tip-toed across the stone slabs, hearing his footfalls like the strike of gongs, hoping the vampires couldn't hear better too. He scrambled towards one set of stone tombs and tried to squeeze himself into one of the sarcophagi, but it was too small for him, and the stone lid would not close. He continued on, searching tombs, until he came to a more elaborate chamber, with a single wooden coffin perched against the wall. He raced over to it and unhinged the lid, jumping back as he saw the creature within.

It was a vampire, but not like any he had seen before, in real life or in film. This was not the romantic kind of Dracula, but the monstrous kind of Nosferatu, an ancient and formidable ancestor of the "modern" families of vampire he had unwittingly encountered. The creature's face was drawn and shrivelled, with gaunt features, showing much of the skull beneath. He had no hair, and his skin seemed to have pulled back so much that his ears had shrunk. He had a large overbite, and from that larger upper jaw protrude long, sharp fangs. His eyes were open, and they were simple black marbles, with not a hint of anything within, but it seemed that he was not awake.

James heard the sounds of the scouting O'Neills behind him, and there was no way out of this chamber other than the way he came. So, in a moment of madness or genius—the outcome deciding which— he stepped into the coffin with the ancient sleeping vampire, pressing himself against the cold, lifeless and shrivelled body, and pulled the lid closed.

At first, he paid little heed of his graveyard bedfellow, for his attention was fixed on the sounds outside. He heard their footsteps loud and clear, and the tremendous echoes of their voices.

"I thought you said you saw something," one of them said.

"I did. It came in here."

"It?"

"Check the coffin."

James' muscles suddenly seized. There was no room to turn or move, and no chance of escape.

"Are you kidding? That's Cían's tomb."

"Lorcan's father?"

"Yes. If you touch that, we can kiss our dreams goodbye. He'll slaughter us all. Probably Lorcan as well."

It was then that James' attention was caught by the vampire he leant against. His face was almost pressed against the drawn skin of Cían's bony cheeks, and his eyes stared straight into the dark, staring eyes of the other. A blade of light sneaked in through a crack in the coffin, just enough to illuminate key features, but not enough to remove those accentuating shadows. James felt no heaving chest beneath him, no twitching of muscles, no tiny shudders of nerves. Yet all through this, he knew in his heart and soul that Cían was alive, that he was merely resting.

Outside, the vampires continued their search for him, growing more and more restless as they came up empty. For James, however, his fears shifted from them to the one he had embraced. He tried to slow his own breathing, so that his own heaving chest might not stir the creature. He tried to turn his head, so that the vampire would not feel his breath. He closed his eyes, but even then he saw those eternally staring pupils. He tried to hold back the horror, to silence a scream. He tried to kill the thought that he had just climbed into his own grave.

CASUS BELLI

It must have been two hours before the O'Neills finally left, abandoning their search for James as the day began to wane—and the Kavanaghs began to wake. James stayed in his coffin hiding place, afraid that even trying to get out might awake the vampire, until Rua came and freed him.

"You are lucky it is I who found you," she told him. "Lorcan might have had your neck."

James loosened his collar. "I think everyone was after my neck."

"This has all the trappings of the O'Neills."

James shrugged. "I never got their names. I was too busy running and screaming."

"Did you see a red-haired woman?"

"No. I saw two big twins though."

"Those are the Brute Brothers. Definitely the O'Neills. They will deny it though. They've done that before when they've broken the rules."

"Can't you punish them?"

Rua sighed, resting her hand on her hip. "I want to, but vampire tradition requires that we need a *casus belli*, a case for war. If the O'Neills deny they were here—and they will have covered their tracks with magic too—then it is largely your word against theirs, and they will argue that we coerced you. If we declare war on the O'Neills, not only will the Gormans and Danestis not come to our raid, they might even be convinced to fight against us. This is what the O'Neills want, a sudden slip-up by us, so that they can swoop in. If they declare war themselves, they will be outmatched. At the least, they want to isolate us, knowing that there are few left of the Kavanagh clan."

They found the beast of Umbra Montis dead on one of the higher levels. Rua ran to it and knelt down, caressing its butchered head. For all its horror—and hers—seeing her tenderness with it made it seem almost endearing.

"They will pay for this," she said.

James couldn't help but feel a little guilty. In many ways, the beast had died saving him. To think that he had feared it only days before.

"What do you plan to do?" James asked.

"We can't afford a war. If we fight them directly, then another family will strike while we are weakened. We need to maintain our authority over them. We need to make it clear that it is the O'Neills who broke the rules."

They heard a rush of footsteps, and saw someone running down the corridor towards them. It was the driver who brought James to this horrible place, and this horrible life he felt he could now not escape from, even if he was no longer locked in his room.

On seeing Rua cradling the head of the beast, the man slowed, then halted, shaking his head. It was only then that James noticed the similarities in his and Rua's features, and thought they must be brother and sister.

"I'll round up the boys," he said, turning back to the stairs.

"No, Caoimh," Rua said, reaching her hand out to stop him.

"They have to pay for this!"

"They will. But let's do this smart."

They found Ebed in the foyer, though only his torso—his head had been ripped clean off, and was nowhere to be found. A trail of blood led to the door, where a scattering of iron nails were left, spelling out the Latin phrase.

"Such destruction," Lorcan pined, shaking his head and seeming horrified by it all. For a vampire, he didn't seem to like the sight of blood all that much.

"Ebed wanted to be turned," Rua said. "We promised that we would in time."

"There are things you can do with the dead," Caoimh suggested.

"No!" Lorcan snapped. "Defile not the dead."

"What's those words written in the blood?" James asked, pointing to the nails, loosely formed into letters by the door.

"*Absit Omen*," Lorcan explained. "*Let an omen be absent*. This was a motto used by the Order of Nails, a group of gypsy vampire-hunters that formed in the absence of the blood wardens."

"What does it mean?"

"It is designed to ward off evil, to ask the Divine—" He stopped to scowl, then regained his composure. "To ask that an event does not turn into a bad omen of more evil to come."

"What it means here," Rua said, "is that the O'Neills are making every effort to hide their footprints. They will claim that it was the Order of Nails that attacked."

"So, what's the plan?" James asked.

It was odd to think it, but he felt more on their side than before. That was the beauty of a common enemy. The O'Neills had hoped to stop him before he got started, but now that he had seen the threat they posed, a part of him—that vampire-hunting part—wanted vengeance. If anything, they had jump-started the process for him.

"They wanted to kill you before you realised your power," Rua told him. "They failed in this attempt, but it is unlikely to be their last. The only way to truly defeat them is for you to become the blood warden you were meant to be."

GARGOYLES

Given the recent events, Rua was in a bad mood. She said she needed to get out of the castle for a bit, "for a breath of fresh air," and directed James to wait outside. It was funny that she didn't expect him to run now. She knew he was just as much in their protection as they claimed to be in his.

While standing outside, he heard the trio of vampires shouting back and forth. It seemed they disagreed strongly on how to proceed. Rua and Lorcan fought the most. For the so-called "perfect marriage" that tradition required, it didn't seem all that perfect.

While he waited, James stared up at the building of Umbra Montis. It was dusk now, but there was still enough light left to highlight its many ancient features. This was the first time he spotted the many gargoyles protruding from the hotel walls, and perched upon its roof. He hadn't really noticed them before in the darkness, but now they were hard to miss. They were all of the same grey stone, with garish faces and fangs bared. Some had wings, and many had claws. All of them had eyes that followed you, and gave you the impression that even if you left the area, they'd follow you still.

"I thought gargoyles were supposed to scare away the demons," James said, when Rua eventually came out alone. By now, the dusk had deepened, but still she lingered in the shadows of the doorway, waiting for the veil of night.

Rua forced a smile. "Not us," she replied. "There are worse things than us in this world, James, and worse still in others. If humans fear vampires, what do vampires fear? What feeds on us?"

"And these protect you?"

"These, and other things. We are at our most vulnerable when we rest, and that is when the dead-eaters would strike, if we did not take precautions."

"You know, you're giving me a lot of information about your weaknesses."

Suddenly she seized him by the throat with her knife-like nails and forced him against the old brickwork. It happened so quickly he barely saw it. He felt it just fine.

"I know yours," she said. "It's called being human."

She let him drop, and he coughed and clutched his neck.

"Some say that's a strength," he replied.

She humphed. "Only humans say that."

He stood up and followed her into the car. "So, what else protects you?"

This time it was a real smile, and a sensual one. "In time … you."

DINNER

Caoimh was the driver once again, but this time James was not alone in the back. Rua sat beside him, one pale leg crossed over the other. Her dress parted almost at the hip, and she sat as poised in the vehicle as she did on her throne, though she didn't wear her crown out here.

It seemed that the vampire queen was lost in thought. She stared out the window, though it was tinted almost completely black. She also moved her fingers through the air as if she was tapping against some invisible table. James could only imagine that it must have been a struggle to resist the provocations of the O'Neill family.

James found himself wandering in his own mind, wondering how he had ended up here. Some of the things his grandmother had told him before now made more sense. She wasn't, as he initially assumed, senile. She had seen and experienced the hidden world, a world which wouldn't remain in hiding for James any longer. He wanted to get away from his dull life. The problem with excitement is that, in this case, it was dangerous.

The car halted outside a restaurant in the City Centre, dubbed Night Bites in neon lights. It looked a bit like an American diner, but something told James that the guests were a little different.

Caoimh opened the door for Rua. He might have been her younger brother (if that really mattered in the endless lives of vampires), but he still treated her like a queen. Maybe it was the Irish in them, or the demon, but those families seemed to look out for each other more than most. Yet maybe it was the uniting effect of another family they could call an enemy.

When Rua rocked her hips up to the entrance of the restaurant, it seemed that everyone inside it noticed. She had a presence that radiated all around her. A flurry of figures came to the front door, holding it open, curtseying to her as she passed.

James followed, but the figures didn't bow to him. They crowded around him, blocking his path. One of them, with tattoos running up his neck, bared his fangs.

"Yo, what blood type is you?" he asked.

"Eh. A."

"Damn. I'm A-intolerant."

"You're what?"

"Ain't got no tolerance for Type A. Didn't I just say that?"

James raised an eyebrow. "What, gives you gas?"

There was a chorus of laughs, and "oohs" and "aahs." These seemed like lowlife gang vampires, unbecoming of the likes of Rua. They didn't radiate the same presence, and they seemed to be making a special effort to be intimidating. The Five Families didn't have to.

"You ever hear a dead guy break wind?" the vampire asked.

"At a morgue once—"

"It ain't pretty, let me tell you that!"

"Boys," Rua interjected, strolling between them like a latin dance. "He's not for eating."

They looked James up and down, clearly wondering what was so special. They never argued with her though, and he was let pass.

"I feel like the turkey that got pardoned," he said.

"Well," she replied. "It isn't Christmas yet."

"Fattening me up?"

She glanced at his chiselled cheeks. "Maybe."

She brought him to a table in the corner, in the shadows. A waiter immediately came over with what an average person might assume was red wine, but James thought it must be blood. Rua gulped it down like an alcoholic.

"It's not the same," she said.

"As what?"

"As drinking straight from the tap."

James almost felt the veins in his neck bulge conspicuously. He adjusted his collar a little, accidentally unearthing the tiny crucifix the airport Garda had given him. Rua's eyes caught sight of it, and she recoiled and snarled at him, holding up a claw to her face, as if she was warding off some evil—or some good.

"Don't wear that thing around me," she barked.

"Sorry, but I don't feel safe without it."

Her glare was penetrating. "You're not safe with it either."

"If it's all the same, I think I'll keep wearing it."

Then her eyes seemed to change, and he felt suddenly paralysed. He had the sensation of falling, except it was like falling forward, straight into the pupils of her eyes, and then drowning there, as if they were an ocean. He heard her speak, but couldn't quite make out the words.

And then he snapped out of it, and found he was wasn't wearing the necklace any more, that he was handing it over to her. She took the little cross between her fingers, which smoked at the touch, and snapped the thing in two.

"I guess you can have it," he said.

"You'll need to learn to resist," she told him. She dropped the two halves of the cross onto the tray of a passing waiter, who almost stumbled when he saw them.

"Maybe you're hard to resist," James replied with a grin.

"But you are not. Your weakness is unattractive."

"Boy," James said. "Talk about rejection."

"The O'Neills will make short work of you if you do not learn to tap into your power soon."

"Yeah, see, about that. I kinda still think you've got the wrong guy."

"Well," she said. "There's a test for that."

"A blood test?"

"Of sorts."

"As long as I don't have to drink any."

She held up her empty glass, licking a stray

droplet from the rim.

"You know not the hunger," she told him earnestly. "You know not the thirst. It overcomes you. It devours you. Whatever humanity we have left is crushed by it, until only the animal is left. When it needs to feed, it must feed. We are on its leash. Where it goes, we must follow. The hunger drives all and consumes all. It is everything. It is life."

"Can you not control it?"

"Some have tried, but most have failed. A few became blood hermits, hiding away from humanity, eating what scraps they could get. They claim great strength in their resistance, but they are but a shadow of themselves. They are not worthy of the name vampire."

"Does no one try to stop you?" he asked, only to realise that probably should be him. "I mean, the government just lets you kill people?"

"Do they have a choice?" she asked in turn.

"Can they not, you know, wipe you out?"

"Can we not wipe them out?"

"Ah."

"That is what they fear, and those of us who have been around long enough to remember the Blood Wars know what it is like if the peace of the vampire clans is broken."

"All hell breaks loose, huh?"

"You could say that. And what peace your kind has will be shattered too."

BALLYBODEN BASTION

In Ballyboden, not far from Kiltipper, the O'Neills had set up their "forward camp," from where they could launch their operations. The Kavanaghs had lodged a complaint about this move at the Red Council, labelling it as an intrusion into their jurisdiction, but the O'Neills dismissed the complaint as a Kavanagh excuse to further deride that noble family.

The O'Neills were building a fortress there, not just to house them, but to provoke the Kavanaghs into a fight. To justify their actions, they used an ancient claim to the land at that location, combined with the vampire tradition of staking such land claims with a building worthy of the family name. It was hard to dispute, and few felt the urge to make a war of words, so often the precursor to a real one.

So Ballyboden fell to the O'Neills without a fight, and the O'Neill clan crept ever closer to Umbra Montis, night by night.

After the recent attempt to extricate James from that castle, the O'Neills retreated to their half-built fortress, where the workers were still busy laying bricks. There was anger among the family at their failure to find the blood warden, and talk of retribution by the Kavanaghs, and fear that they had not covered their tracks well enough.

Dearg was defiant, but even as she swore to her kin that the Kavanaghs would do nothing, she was alerted to a visitor on the horizon. She went to the parapets, where she saw Caoimh approaching.

"This is an intrusion," she shouted down at him.

His voice rocked the heavens. "*This* is? What do you have to say about the attack you made on Umbra Montis?"

She tried to disguise her smile. "What attack?"

"We know it was you."

"That's quite an accusation. Fighting words, even. Did you come here for a fight?"

"No," he replied, "but it seems you came to my home seeking a war."

"Is that a declaration of it?"

"It's a statement of the facts. You can lie now, but sooner or later the truth will come out."

"Sooner or later," she replied. "Maybe you'll get your war."

"You're not the only magic user out there. We can have a truth-finder after you."

"You shouldn't make threats," Dearg said. Her hand sparked with magical energy. "Does Rua even know you're here?"

"Consider this a warning," Caoimh said. "There's a reason why my family rules."

"All empires fall."

Caoimh retreated, driving back towards the

restaurant where he had left Rua and James. Maggie O'Neill asked Dearg if she should follow him, but Dearg felt it was better not to push their luck with him. She had a different plan in mind.

"We need to do something," Maggie said. "The blood warden will only get stronger."

"He's strong enough already," their uncle Kieran added, "even if he doesn't know it yet."

"Everyone has a weakness," Dearg said. "Sometimes it's someone else."

DEAD AND LONELY

"Tell me something," James said. "Are these other guests here members of your family?"

"No," Rua replied. "There are few true members of the Five Families. These here are a lesser breed of vampire. We have an agreement with the government to keep their numbers down, a blood quota, if you will. Because the Kavanagh clan is waning, we are allowed to fill our ranks with these types, but they are a pale shadow of the true vampire."

"They look pretty nasty to me."

"Looks can be very deceiving, James. By bolstering our numbers, we seem strong, but the ruling family is weak. There's no point lying about it to you. The other families see it, and some are ready to pounce. It's why we need you to be the strength we lack."

James didn't reply to that. He'd been hearing a lot about his apparent strength, but hadn't felt any of it himself. He wasn't sure what to say. He also wasn't sure how long he'd last if they discovered he wasn't who they thought he was.

"Are you hungry?" Rua asked him.

James glanced around at the other diners, all of them having a liquid lunch. "I think I've lost my appetite."

"This place also serves human food."

"Is that human food, or is the food human?"

She cocked her head and raised her eyebrows. He thought maybe a sense of humour didn't survive the grave.

"So, why here?" he asked. "Why not dine back at the ho—eh, castle."

"Because Lorcan is there."

"Is that not a good thing?"

She stared at him, and her eyes showed pain.

"No?" he said after a brief silence.

"They say it's lonely at the top, but it's even lonelier when you're up there with someone you feel no connection with. I am living a lie. Now I know what it feels like to pretend to be in a happy marriage for the sake of the children, but I do this not for my own, for I have none, and never shall. I do this for the children of men."

"Can the dead even be lonely?" James asked.

"I'm only dead on the outside. I can still feel. Emotion doesn't end with death. Normally those emotions disperse, and sometimes they fixate on a location, but with the undead they fixate on the corpse. They stay with us, just like everything else, animated by the hidden rules governing nature, of which the magicians have long sought."

She reached across the table, grasping his hand in hers. The grip was like a vice, even though it seemed like she was trying to be gentle. She stared into his eyes, and she seemed suddenly less grim, now a little vulnerable.

"I'm lonely, James. You have no idea how it feels. There is the loneliness of the living, which hurts a thousand hurts. But the loneliness of the dead, it hurts a million more. Those you care for perish, and you wish your feelings perished with them, but they go on. If anything, they get stronger. The pain, the hurt, the loneliness—it all gets stronger."

"So, immortality isn't all it's cracked up to be, huh?"

"No. There are pros, don't get me wrong, but there are cons too."

"You have Lorcan."

She laughed, though it wasn't a mirthful laugh. "I don't *have* Lorcan, nor does he have me. We don't have each other. We have nothing but a charade, a display. We have the 'perfect marriage' that tradition bids us have, but we only have it in name, not in heart. It is not perfect, and it is barely a marriage at all. It is a bond of convenience, a link of necessity, that we might rule, and so put an end to those dark days of the past. But it is all a ruse, and people are seeing that now."

"Why don't you end it?"

"I want to, and maybe I work against myself to make it so. But this is bigger than us. For us, there are more important things."

She paused, glancing around the room to see if anyone was in earshot, then looked at James. "You know, he doesn't even like women."

"Could've fooled me," James replied, remembering

how fondly Lorcan seemed to look at Rua.

"Anyone could fool you."

"Sheesh."

"I'm not even sure why I'm telling you all of this. I guess I've kept it bottled up for so long. The Danestis came together with my family to organise a peace across Europe, not just here. Lorcan comes from those treaties, not from love. We saw the threat of war on the horizon—and two world wars spawned on this continent soon after—but they would have been nothing compared to the war of worlds we would be waging if we hadn't settled those old family feuds. The Danestis married into a variety of families across Europe so that they could have a say in our affairs, a place at the table, as it were. They were outnumbered by the Draculestis, of whom our own Dublin-born Bram Stoker made so popular in fiction, but with the pattern of allegiances the Danestis formed, they soon outmatched their most hated rivals. Stoker was lucky he found the protection of friends in the Order of the Golden Dawn, for the Danestis despised him and his focus on the Dracul name. They were able to rile up many families over Stoker's publishing of vampire secrets, so that even his descendants are in need of magical warding today."

"Wow," James said. "And here I was thinking it was all fiction."

"The barrier between fact and fiction is more blurred than you think."

"Yeah, I can see that now."

"But you still don't see your own power."

"Umm, that's ... a little harder to see, yeah."

Rua stood up suddenly. "Come with me."

James followed her through the kitchen at the back and out into a dark alleyway.

"What do you see here?" she asked.

He peered into the darkness, but saw nothing.

"You have trained yourself to be blind," she said, "like so many humans have. I suppose it's a way to stay sane in an insane world."

"I guess it's too late for me then," James said.

"Yes," she replied, a little colder than before.

He turned to her, but she wasn't there. He heard the clang of the metal door behind him, and the sound of a lock sliding into place.

Then, as he turned back to the shadows, he began to see. There was a vampire there, approaching slowly, his eyes filled with hunger, and his fangs ready for the taste.

A TASTE

The vampire seized James by the shoulder and hurled him against the wall. The impact winded him, and he wheezed as he slumped to the ground. He barely had time to fully feel the pain, however, for the vampire lunged at him again, hauling him to his feet.

At that moment, when James saw the fangs glimmering in the moonlight, and the snarling face, and the red eyes, he thought that it was all over, that his brief experience with the supernatural world was coming to an end. If he was lucky—or unlucky—he could get to hang around as a ghost.

The vampire tore at the collar of his shirt, sending a button spinning off into the air. Had he still worn the little crucifix, the beast might have been warded off, or at least slowed a little. But there was no chain now, and even the mark the talisman made in his neck was quickly fading. There was no obstacle left between those sharpened fangs and his tender throat.

Then, as the fangs came close, James found his reflexes kicking in. He moved his arms to block his face, then found himself instinctively twisting out of the vampire's grasp, despite the strength of the creature's grip. He spun under the vampire's arm, turning on the spot, and casting the vampire against the wall.

Then he backed away, stumbling, feeling suddenly the pain that he had not felt before. He panted, and his heart bashed against his ribs, as if it had become an ally of the undead. He held his arms out before him, ready for the next attack, while his eyes searched out any avenue of escape. There was none.

The vampire turned, slowly, hunching its back, and snarled even more.

"You fight," he said, surprised.

James was not surprised by that. He was surprised he fought so well.

"The blood is sweeter after a struggle," the vampire taunted.

Then it charged at him, moving faster than any human could. Though James tried to dodge the attack, the vampire caught hold of him and pulled him to the ground. It loomed over him, and clawed at him, and James clawed back.

Yet no matter what hidden well of fortitude James found within him, the vampire had a supernatural strength that soon overcame him. It pinned his arms, kneeling on top of them, holding him down, until all James could do was wait.

Then he felt the pierce, the bite. It was such a sharp, sudden pain, that it paralysed him. He opened his mouth to give a cry, but merely caught his own breath. Then he felt that horrible extraction, like the suction of the needle when giving blood. The vampire drank, and drank, until James felt he was going to pass out. Any fight in him vanished, just as it was needed most.

This was the end. Another sip and he was gone.

And yet, the vampire stopped.

Dazed, James turned his head, and he realised the vampire was moving away, and stumbling. It fell over, and got back to its feet, then collapsed again. That should have been him. That should have been his stumble home, or to the hospital, or to the morgue.

James struggled up a little, onto his elbow, just enough to get a better look. Even as he did, he realised he probably should have been playing dead. Maybe the vampire thought he'd had his fill, that there was no more blood to give.

No.

The vampire clawed at itself, cutting great gashes across its skin with its nails. Through those wounds, it looked like it was on fire inside. It screamed, and the cry was blood-curdling, if you had enough blood left to curdle. Its skin blistered and burned, and it patted and clawed at it. Its body smoked, but even through the steam you could see the horror of it all. The vampire crumbled apart like ash, and you could see the skeleton beneath, until there were no more screams, and very little left at all.

James felt like vomiting, but he was too weak even for that. He heard the clang and screech of the metal door opening, and the clap of heels against the ground. He saw Rua's black shoes, and pale legs, and red dress. He could almost see her black heart.

"You," he said, but it was a struggle.

"No," she said. "You. You did this." She gestured to the vampire's remains.

"I don't understand."

"I knew you wouldn't believe me if I told you. So I showed you. You're stronger than you think. You don't need trinkets and baubles to fend off my kind. No. Your blood is poison to us."

"I don't—"

"Don't worry," she said, and she was convincing. "You'll recover sooner than most. You're a hardy type. An ancient line. There are not many of your kind left. We killed most of them, until the truce."

"And now?"

"Now you call a truce of your own. Or," and she paused, running the side of her index finger across her lower lip, so that her fangs dinged the skin, "you kill most of us." Yet she clearly wasn't talking about herself.

INVASION

Lilly was having a quiet Sunday, curling up by the fire with a good book. A magic book, of course. Until she was accepted by a coven, this was her only avenue to learn. It was risky to learn this way without the guidance of someone more experienced, but she didn't have the patience the wait.

She was just at a really interesting section on invocations when there was a tremendous thump at the door. She perked up, wondering if maybe it was James. She hadn't been able to get through to his mobile, and he hadn't met her for lunch. She listened for another sound. It came swiftly with a thunderous clap. This wasn't someone knocking. It was someone trying to get in.

She leapt out of her seat and ran to the door, just as it splintered open.

There, on the other side, stood the O'Neills, with Dearg front and centre, both arms outstretched, as if to announce "I'm here!"

"You can't come in," Lilly blurted. "You're not invited."

Dearg smiled and tapped a bladed fingernail against the invisible barrier. It shimmered electric blue. Then she looked at the book Lilly was still clutching in her hands.

"You're a witch, huh?"

Lilly said nothing.

"Well," Dearg continued. "I know some magic too."

With that, the vampire immediately began an incantation, and though Lilly was still unschooled in much of magic, she knew instantly that it was a barrier-breaking spell. Normally this wasn't something you had to worry about with vampires. But not Dearg. She was unique.

Lilly thought for a moment that she might escape from the window, but she knew the vampires would be waiting for her there. They could outrun her with ease. When in a siege, the defender usually had the advantage. But only if the walls held.

She grabbed her mobile phone and called for James. "Come on, pick up," she pleaded. It rang out. She tried again, but it went straight to voicemail. She didn't want to think about what might have happened to him. If it was bad, she was probably going to find out first-hand.

She glanced back at the broken door, where the barrier was breaking. She could see, just on the edge of vision, the glimmer of a giant battering ram, with the face of a gargoyle. Dearg rocked back and forth like the tide, throwing her arms forward for the punch of the ram, then drawing them back to prepare for another strike. The barrier could only take so much of this.

Lilly frantically searched through her bookcase for some defensive tomes, knocking normally prized books to the floor in the panic of it all. She wasn't even sure what she was looking for, and grabbed the first volume she could find with some protective magic. She cast it open and raced about the room to find her supplies. She got several items on the list, running her shaking finger down the page, until she got to "the heart of a virgin child."

"Damn," she said, sighing.

The barrier was weakening. She could see the glimmering light flicker, like a candle burning low.

So she grabbed another book, one she would only use as a last resort. She thought this might qualify. It was a demonic grimoire, with depictions of all kinds of horrible, twisted creatures with many heads and the wrong bodies parts, hybrids of human and animal, and things beyond imagination. She poured a salt circle around her, unsure if that would do, and flicked through the pages until she got to the one she remembered: *Evocation of a Dead-eater*.

She read the strange text, the so-called "barbarous words of invocation." Her voice changed mid-way through, deepening and darkening. The lights flickered and dulled. It almost seemed like clouds were forming in the room.

The barrier broke, and the vampires stormed in. Dearg walked, but the others ran, charging straight for Lilly. Salt wouldn't hold them back.

But a Dead-eater would.

Just as they neared Lilly, everything went pitch

black, as if they had been sucked into a black hole. Yet that would have been a mercy. Instead, something came out of one. Lilly felt a sudden fear like nothing she had felt before, worse than anything, worse than what she felt from the vampires. Maybe it was because she felt their fear too.

The light flickered just enough to see a mangled shape, constantly changing, an arm reaching out of a giant mouth, a mouth forming in the palm of the hand. It was all a twisted mess of nightmares, but it was real, and it was here.

The creature seized the closest vampire, Feargal, and consumed him. His cries carried on even after he was gone, as if he was now being consumed for eternity. Lilly almost had pity. Almost.

Dearg swiftly formed her own barrier between her and the Dead-eater, but she didn't stay long to test it out. She launched herself through the nearest window and fled. The other surviving members of her family quickly followed, but the slowest of them, Mark, was caught in what seemed like a vacuum suction, pulled by the intake of the Dead-eater's breath. He reached out to grab onto something, but everything gave way in his hands. Lilly's apartment was falling apart, becoming just another meal for the monster. With it, it gulped down Mark O'Neill too.

Then it was just the two of them, her and the demon. It turned to her without turning, a kind of face appearing in its back, if it had a back. An eye appeared and stared at her. She was alive, and had a soul. That wasn't what the Dead-eaters feasted on. But as it looked at her, and filled her with a terror of thousands of consumed creatures, she suddenly didn't feel so sure.

She looked at her salt circle. It didn't seem adequate for this at all. She wasn't even sure if that held it at bay, or if it just didn't like the look of her. The feeling was mutual. She patted her pockets for her phone, but spotted it on the bookshelf nearby—outside the circle. She knew enough about magic to know not to leave it, not to even reach a hand outside.

She was safe, for now. For what little training she had, she had succeeded at one of the hardest invocations. The threat of death was a great motivator. The problem was that she never really learned any banishing. She got the Dead-eater here, but she didn't know how to get it back.

GRAVEYARD CHASE

Dearg ran, and the Dead-eater followed, launching itself out of Lilly's apartment, seeming to fall apart as it did, only to reassemble itself in the alley outside. The O'Neill family split apart in all directions, using their unnatural speed to get away. But it wasn't chasing them. It was hungry for her.

She raced through the alleyway, aware that the strain of the magic she had used had already slowed her down. She had prepared to feed. She hadn't prepared to be the meal.

The swirling mass of mouths and arms and God-knows-what came in pursuit. It had its own kind of unnatural swiftness, but it was less movement and more a form of teleportation through tiny vortexes. A limb would disappear into one, and then came out of another further ahead. So it seemed to disassemble itself, or maybe it was pulled apart, only to reform further ahead.

Dearg leapt up onto the bonnet of a car, and then hopped across the roofs of several vehicles, trying to remember some spell for speed. Fear fuelled her feet quite well, but that same fear told her that it was not enough.

As the Dead-eater followed, the cars were left mangled in its wake, just as twisted as it was. There might have been people in some of them. They weren't people any more. The Dead-eater hungered for the lifeless and rotting, but it consumed the living in its path as well.

Dearg's heels clattered off the cobblestones. Her hair whipped the wind and lashed her face. Just as easily as Lilly summoned the Dead-eater, Dearg's mind summoned those few fears she felt. She remembered every time she closed her coffin lid, and that brief feeling of vulnerability at the thought of what was out there, circling like vultures in some demonic plane of existence. Here it was, the nightmare unleashed.

She made for the nearest graveyard, sensing its location, feeling the death in there. But the Dead-eater hungered for the living dead, not just a corpse. The graves alone would not do.

The gate was ahead, but the beast was behind. As she closed the gap, so did it. Then, as she made a leap to clear the wall, she felt a sudden revulsion and was forced back. This was hallowed ground. She wasn't welcome there.

If she had time, she could have worked her magic against that barrier, but it was strong. She didn't have time. If she wasn't quick, she wouldn't have anything at all.

So she ran again, alongside the cemetery wall. The brickwork buckled behind her as the darkness followed. She recited old words and made signs with her hand, before making a gesture like grabbing the head of a vegetable and pulling it from the earth.

Inside the graveyard, something stirred. The ground shuddered in one spot, and then a decaying hand broke through. *Muriel Conroy. Wife and mother. Gone too soon.* Back even sooner.

The Dead-eater halted and raised its head, if you could call it a head. Its bulbous, bloated form seemed to collapse into itself and then push out something with a mouth, which gave the most ghastly intake of breath, like someone gasping for air. It was its own kind of sniffing something out, and it smelled the dead arise beyond the wall.

Dearg kept running, slowing for nothing. She cast the spell again, and another arm broke loose, followed by its late owner.

The wall crumbled as the Dead-eater passed on through. The shambling form of Muriel Conroy, casting a haze of dust behind her, was its target. Yet Dearg knew that it was just an appetiser. Once it was done with Muriel, it would be back for the main course. She needed to fill it up. She wasn't sure if the graveyard had enough bodies for that, or if she had enough magic in her to raise them all. But she gave it her best.

The graveyard rocked. Headstones tilted, and some were felled like dominoes. Entire rows of graves burst to life, and the dead arose, dazed and hungry. They ignored the token tributes of their loved ones, stomped on the flowers, and left behind mounds of muck to mar their engraved names. Then the Dead-eater got to them, and they wished they were really dead.

ON THE ROAD

Rua brought James out to where Caoimh should have been parked, but it took about fifteen minutes for the car to arrive. The glare she gave the driver would have eroded rocks.

The journey back to Umbra Montis was even grimmer for James than it ever was before. Knowing about vampires was bad enough. Feeling one suck the blood—and the life—out of you was something else entirely. That he had been served up "to prove a point" didn't help either.

"It was necessary," was all Rua would say on the matter. She sat in the back of the car with him, tall and intimidating, while Caoimh drove silently, seeming like he had been lashed by some invisible whip.

"I think I would've believed you," James said.

"I know you wouldn't have, not like you believe experience. That was only, if you forgive the phrase, a *taste* of how powerful you really are. I couldn't afford to wait for you to discover it by yourself. Your power is locked away. I had to begin picking the lock."

"Well, you know," James replied, "maybe *I* can do

that."

She stared at him, and he suddenly felt transfixed, unable to move, or do anything. Everything except her faded to black.

Then she looked away, and the paralysis ended.

"You can't even resist the vampire gaze," she scolded. "You needed to be stronger, and you need to be stronger soon."

"This is all new to me. I … I need time to let it sink in."

"If you give it too much time, it'll be the fangs that sink in."

"Well, at least they'll die if they try, right?"

"If they feast for long enough. The strongest of us can endure a sup."

James didn't like that thought. The Red Council had shown him that there were quite a few strong vampires in the country.

"Maybe he's not the answer to our problems," Caoimh suggested.

The feeling in the car changed, and James felt suddenly worried for the driver.

"Where were you?" Rua asked.

"I just went for a spin," Caoimh responded.

"Did you go to Ballyboden?"

"No, of course not."

There was a pause, where Rua chewed her lip. It seemed like she was going to burst out into a fit of anger, but before she could say anything, Caoimh pointed ahead.

"There's something on the road," he said, his voice hush.

James might have expected Rua to say something like "Go around it," but she grew suddenly alert. There was enough in Caoimh's tone to tell her that it was serious, that it was bad. She leant forward, casting her gaze out into the road ahead. James could barely see anything in the darkness, but she could see something that made her hand tremble just a little.

James didn't see it, and had no word for it, but it was clear to Rua what stood out there in the road: a Dead-eater.

"Turn around!" she cried.

Caoimh twisted the wheel sharply, but they kept their current course. "I can't," he said, barely audible. His hands shook much more than Rua's. He clutched the wheel not to drive, but to settle the shakes.

"Then accelerate," she told him.

Caoimh complied, pressing hard on the accelerator. The car zoomed forward, until the headlights gave form to the creature that barely had any. It was such a fleeting glimpse, and such a shifting form, that James wasn't even sure what he had seen.

Rua turned to him. "If you survive this—"

Then the car struck the creature, and everything turned to chaos. The speed of the impact should have toppled anything not bolted to the ground, but instead if was like hitting a wall. Everyone inside was thrown forward, and would have been thrown further if their seatbelts did not yank them back. The back wheels rose, and then the whole car flipped, until the ground was the sky, and the Dead-eater was some dark god that dwelt there. Glass smashed, and shards of it spread throughout the vehicle, stabbing and slicing. The somersaulting car landed on the roof, and gravity played tug of war with their seatbelts. Cut and bruised, and altogether dazed, the survivors of the crash stirred inside. Outside was another survivor, slinking slowly towards them.

"Get out," Rua urged. She sliced through her seatbelt with her razor-sharp nails, tumbling down, and still seeming somehow elegant when she did it.

James fumbled with his own harness, but his own weight made it difficult to free himself. He tugged at the buckle, and tried to reach the release switch, all the while seeing the Dead-eater slither towards them, leaving behind a kind of slime made of shadow.

Rua kicked open one of the doors, then freed James with a flurry of nails. He barely had time to fall before she started to pull him out. He stumbled, and she faltered with him. If her grace was infectious, so was his lack of it.

"Get out, Caoimh!" she cried.

The driver stirred inside, pulling off his broken sunglasses. He looked through the windscreen. The Dead-eater was very close now.

"Go," he said, resigned. "I'll slow it down."

"You won't," she hissed. "Get out. Come, Caoimh. Run!"

But it was too late. The Dead-eater reached the car, and what wasn't already buckled started to give way before it. It made its terrible sigh, like a muted banshee wail, and Caoimh was pulled back in his seat. Only the straining belt held him in place. He didn't even try to hold on.

Rua pulled James to his feet, and grabbed his

chin, twisting his head towards her. She pulled him close, close enough that he would feel her breath, if she ever had one. "Go," she told him, and it was more than just a plea. She used her hypnotic gaze to make it harder to ignore. "Find safety. Find help. Just go. Run. Get out of here!"

He started to leave, but his steps were slow. He didn't even know where he was going. The loss of blood and the crash had taken a lot out of him. She told him to run, and he tried to obey, but right now all he could do was walk.

Then he glanced back, even as he continued his slow retreat, and he saw Rua dashing towards the front of the car, where the Dead-eater continued to suck Caoimh out of his seat. She grasped the handle of the door, but a tentacle of shadow and ooze lashed at her hand, and she gave a dreadful cry, pulling her hand black, where it seemed that black veins spread inside.

"It's too late," Caoimh said, as the threads in the strap became undone. "I'm not worth dying for."

"You're worth living for," Rua replied, and she grabbed the handle tight. The lash came again, and the tentacle stayed. She gritted her teeth through the pain, letting her scream break through the gaps in her teeth. She pulled the door off, wrenching her hand free from the Dead-eater's grasp.

She reached in to Caoimh, and their hands met. Then several arms reached out of the torso of the Dead-eater and grabbed Rua, holding her in a demonic bear hug. She wailed in agony, as if she was being torn apart inside.

Caoimh looked at her with tears in his eyes. She should have run. Now both of them would perish in the most horrible way known to the undead.

Then, just as it all seemed over, and James tried to look away, a light shone in the darkness. Out of that light stepped Mr. Constant, who pulled a wand from his inside coat pocket.

A LIGHT IN THE DARKNESS

Mr. Constant stepped forward, and with the flick of his wrist he launched a projectile made of light at the Dead-eater. It struck its body, and the creature recoiled and cried out, with many new mouths forming all over it to add to the terrible cry.

Mr. Constant raised the wand over his head, spinning it swiftly, as if to charge it with even more power, before pointing it at the creature again. This time a larger stream of light shot forth, hitting not only the Dead-eater, but the car as well. Rua scowled and sneered at the sudden illumination, raising her arm to shield her eyes. She pulled Caoimh from the wreckage with even greater speed, fleeing into the shadows, where James watched the battle unfold.

The Dead-eater let out a terrible roar, like a battle cry. It faced the magician, and though it was in pain—and perhaps always was—it seemed to be preparing for an attack.

The magician kept up his barrage of glowing missiles, advancing as he did. They tore off bits of the creature, but the parts that fell seemed to become little monsters of their own. Some started to worm their way towards him, until he blasted them apart, and others floated through the air, until he destroyed those too.

Then the Dead-eater used the black holes from which it came as a means of attack. A portal opened beside it, through which it stretched a swiftly-growing arm. Another opening appeared behind the magician, from which the arm appeared, grasping Mr. Constant's shoulder and eliciting a cry from him. He broke away from it, and a shimmer of light formed around him in a globe, but the grip left a black stain on his coat.

Again the Dead-eater reached into the nothingness and grasped from a different place. It was all arms, appearing out of nowhere, feeling through the darkness of the night, trying to maul the magician, trying to grab him and strangle him. It seemed to take a great effort on Mr. Constant's part to evade all of these, for they came with no warning, and even his own shield of light began to strain.

Then Mr. Constant held out his left hand towards the beast, and pointed the wand straight towards the heavens, where it glowed. He took a deep breath, the kind that took years of meditation to master, and uttered a Latin phrase that rocked the ground and rent the heavens.

"Procul, O Procul, Este Profani!"

There was a blast of light, blinding and burning. James thought he would never see again, and the vampires gave out a cry of pain that matched the one given by the demon. When the light subsided, and his sight returned, James saw a wave of energy pushing the Dead-eater back, not just back upon the ground, but back into a dark portal to its own realm. It grasped at the ground, and grew more arms to reach out for something to cling to, but the light continued to force it back until it was no more.

Mr. Constant let out an audible, angry sigh. He looked at James, and the two vampires hiding behind him, using his shadow for cover from the light.

"Who brought this here?" the magician shouted.

Rua emerged, still shielding her eyes with her hands, though now the fingers were splayed, so that she looked between the barbed nails.

"You know I do not mess with that world," she stated.

"And Caoimh?"

"I do what she does," Caoimh said, "or doesn't do."

"Well," Mr. Constant said, walking up to James, "I doubt it was you."

"Yeah, I think you can rule me out."

"But what about Lilly?"

"Lilly? You know Lilly?"

"Know her?" Mr. Constant asked, raising his eyebrows. "Dear Lord, that girl will be the death of me."

Rua glowered at him. "If she keeps this up, she'll be the death of us all."

ONE GRAIN AT A TIME

Lilly was relieved when the Dead-eater left her apartment, but her relief didn't last very long. It left a little something behind—a lot of little somethings. As she stood trembling in the circle of salt, half a dozen little blobs, which fell from the creature previously, snailed their way towards her.

"Go away!" she cried. "Shoo!" She made a shooing gesture, but dared not leave the circle.

The first of the blobs reached the salt. A mouth formed in it, and out of it stretched a blackened tongue. It lapped up a single grain, seeming to enjoy the saltiness, and then reached out for another. The other blobs joined it, feasting on the salt.

If Lilly had had training, or even read further in her books, she might have known what to do. She might even have known whether or not these creatures could harm her, or whether the salt barrier she had erected was any kind of barrier at all. All she could think of while she stood there was that when the circle was broken, or there was no more salt to eat, they would try to eat her. Or worse—the Dead-eater itself would come back.

Maybe it was luck—or fate—but, for some arcane reason, the blobs did not cut straight through one part, but ate in concentric circles, gobbling up each layer one at a time. This delayed the breaking of the barrier, but if death was coming anyway, delay just amounted to torture.

The salty circle was very thin now, just three or four grains thick. Lilly held her hands together, a kind of subconsciousness act of prayer. She wondered if this ending would be worse than what the vampires had in store for her. She had been warned to be careful with magic. She never really heeded those warnings.

The final layer was left for one of the blobs, while the others gathered around, baring their teeth. They were very small, about the size of a tennis ball, but she had no racket to bash them away, and tennis balls didn't bite.

She knew that the end was coming, and she resolved to fight. She would kick at them, even if in doing so they snapped off her toes between those razor maws. She would thrash them with her hands, even if they nipped off the tips of her fingers, and gnawed them down to the knuckles. She wouldn't go easily. Just like the grains, they'd have to take her one little bit at a time.

Then she heard a clamour of footsteps up the stairs, and into the room burst Mr. Constant, brandishing his copper-plated blasting rod. He barely even glanced upon the tiny creatures before he flicked blade of light at each of them in turn, shouting aloud, "Procul!" They evaporated into the nothingness of the void, and a rain of salt fell from the ceiling, as if their bellies were emptied in the process.

"Curses, child!" Mr. Constant barked.

Lilly was no child, but twenty-one years hadn't given her much of wisdom yet, and compared to the wizened form of that cranky magician, most were children.

James ran to Lilly, pulling her close, calming her trembling limbs. She hadn't realised that she was crying until she felt the tears moisten the material on James' shoulder.

Mr. Constant kicked his way through some of the fallen books by the bookcase, until he saw the tome known as the *Malum Malignum*. He swept it up and wrapped it inside his coat pocket.

"You shouldn't even *have* this!" he yelled.

"It's lucky I did!" Lilly shouted back.

"Lucky? Do you know what these things can do?"

"I was finding out."

"You were finding out the hard way. The wrong way."

"Well, it's the only way I know."

"And you wonder why the Order rejected your application? You're reckless, child. Foolish and reckless. Magic isn't a game."

"I know," she protested.

"Well, it's time you stop treating it like one."

James patted Lilly on the shoulder in reassurance, but he regretted drawing the ire of Mr. Constant in the process.

"And you," the librarian growled. "It's time you stop playing at being a vampire hunter and start acting like one. The time for child's play is over. We've had the first battle. There's a war on the horizon. You better arm yourself."

THE TRIAL OF THE CROSS

They didn't stay long at Lilly's apartment, for fear that the O'Neills would return—though even they would have been reluctant to return to the site where a Dead-eater appeared. There was a horrible, dark feeling left in the place, as if somehow there was still something there, gnawing at your soul.

Mr. Constant brought his car, and drove them out of Dublin. Caoimh sat in the front passenger seat, eyeing the magician with suspicion. He could feel the wards he had in place. They were strong.

It was a little crowded in the back. Lilly sat between James and Rua, and the vampire cast a disgusted glance at the witch every now and then.

"I can smell the magic off you," she said.

"We all can," Mr. Constant scolded, casting a glance in the mirror. He could only see two people in the back.

"Where are we going anyway?" James asked.

"To get you a weapon."

"The Cross of St. Benedict," Rua said, snarling partway through. Caoimh joined her in an involuntary growl.

"A grave and terrible weapon," Mr. Constant explained, "to ward off the terrible creatures of the grave. It was last used a hundred years ago, when the blood wardens were still active, before this long peace made us a little too comfortable. It was hidden away to keep it safe."

"So, it's like a talisman?" Lilly asked.

"Less thought of talismans from you!" the magician replied. "But yes, a talisman of protection, and a weapon of warding. And most of all, a reminder of the power of the blood warden, which James needs the most."

"I guess it can't hurt to have a weapon," James said.

Rua scoffed. "It'll hurt a lot just trying to get it."

THE PASSAGE TOMB

Mr. Constant drove for several hours before they arrived at a passage tomb, one of the unmarked locations that linked up with Newgrange, but was not open to visitors. Some people broke through the barriers to see it, mostly pagans looking to conduct a ritual, and they often reported feeling a dark energy there. This was why.

"Below this mound is a network of challenges," Rua said. "They are designed to deter any but a true blood warden. No vampires may enter, and even standing this close, I am repulsed by it. Even a magician as strong as Ernest Constant will be of little aid."

"I'm kind of wishing it was just a written test," James replied.

"You won't be joking in there," Mr. Constant said.

"Yeah. That's what I'm afraid of."

"You'll be fine," Rua reassured him.

"Is 'fine' enough, though?"

"If it's not, you'll find more. The will of a blood warden is inexhaustible. It is a well from which an endless water pours. You have let the world dull your senses. You have let your work quench the fires within you. This challenge will unleash your true potential."

Her words were encouraging, but Mr. Constant had to intrude with his dour interjection.

"I should warn you though," he said. "You may die here."

James raised an eyebrow. "Yeah, thanks for that."

"I'm obligated to be honest."

"And here I was thinking you were all about oaths of silence."

The magician humphed. "I'll shut up if you go inside."

They approached the entrance, where a boulder had been rolled aside, but James hesitated.

"Once inside," Mr. Constant said, "this entrance seals, and the only way out is at the very end. We'll be waiting for you there."

James look at the small round opening and gulped.

"I can't do this," he said. "I … just can't. This isn't who I am. I'm not brave like you guys. I'm just a man."

"There's no such thing," Mr. Constant replied. "You can't be *just* a man, for that is an oxymoron. To be a man is to be something more than mere mortal. Humanity was given gifts that even the gods desire. Freedom is one of them. Free will is our curse and our salvation. Right now, you have the choice to become more, or become less."

James sighed. "Then I guess I become less."

Mr. Constant's face went red. He suddenly pulled loose the tie he was wearing and wrapped it around

James' neck, tying the knot quickly, shimmying it up until he was almost choking.

"Is this what you want?" he shouted at him. "To go back to your old life? You might as well tie the noose yourself!"

James tried to pull it open, but the magician yanked it tight again.

"You have good and evil here, coming together for a greater good. I bet you didn't know that, that a lesser evil could help further the cause of the greater good. But a lesser good, through inaction, can also help further the cause of a greater evil."

Those words played heavy on James' heart. He knew deep down that he was destined for this, even if he wasn't entirely sure he believed in destiny. But this wasn't about belief; it was about knowing—and he knew that everything they told him to date was true, especially what they told him about himself. What he didn't like was that he learned some other things, like how much of a coward he really was. It was one thing to talk about adventure, and quite another to live it.

"Okay," he said. It was hardly a declaration of enthusiasm, but from him it was a lot, a start, a step in the right direction. It didn't matter if the steps were small or slow, only that he was taking them. Yet it seemed that the impending vampire war was pushing him on a little faster than he was ready for.

"Is that a yes?" Mr. Constant asked.

James offered his tie back to the magician.

"Keep it," Mr. Constant said. "I have a feeling you might be needing it."

If anything, that propelled James on more than

anything. It was a slight to him, a sign that the magician had no confidence in him, that he thought he'd be back in his old office job after this. James didn't so much get courage from that, but defiance, but it didn't really matter, so long as it pushed him through the door.

He hung the tie around his shoulders loosely, then turned to face the entrance to the passage tomb.

"I guess this is it," he said.

Lilly hugged him tightly.

"Stay safe," she urged. She dropped a little talisman into his shirt pocket and patted his chest there to make him feel it. She'd offered him protection charms when he was in the States, but he always refused. He didn't refuse this one.

He took a step forward, towards that ancient door, perhaps towards his doom. Before he could change his mind—and his mind was already changing— Rua pushed him through. He stumbled through the archway, and felt the tingling of the barrier as he passed between those stone pylons. He turned to look back, but a large stone rolled into place, sealing him inside.

The only way out now was through the gauntlet. He didn't know it, but even if he died there, his ghost could never leave. He either got out alive or didn't get out at all.

THE GAUNTLET

James looked ahead at the dark passage leading deep down into the earth. He felt he'd spent far too much time descending beneath the ground. It kind of felt a little like digging his own grave.

He took the torch from his belt, a parting gift from his new accomplices, and turned it on. It was a battery-powered beam, which he suddenly thought looked a little out of place for such an ancient location, but so long as the light stayed on, he didn't mind. He just hoped that whatever guardians this place had wouldn't mind either.

He took one cautious step forward, testing the dusty ground with the toes of his foot. He wasn't sure what he was expecting, but he'd seen enough films to expect *something*. But nothing happened. That worried him more than anything, but then maybe this wasn't a physical challenge, but a challenge for the mind, or maybe the soul.

He continued on, shining the light everywhere ahead of him, then turning sharply when he heard the tumble of scree behind. There was nothing there.

It was probably just the shifting of the stones, like the creaking of an old mansion. A new fear blossomed in his mind: that this ancient structure could collapse on him. It'd be a cruel irony to fear supernatural threats, but be killed by Nature instead.

He stalked his way through the chamber, his eyes darting in all directions. He saw depictions on the walls, like a halfway point between the crude drawings of the cavemen and the elaborate art of the Egyptians. They seemed to tell a story, but it wasn't a good story; it wasn't something that'd help you get asleep at night. It showed the monsters coming from across the sea, and the death and destruction that came with them. It showed those who fought, and died, and the many wars that followed. It showed bearers of the light, guardians against the shadow. It showed good and evil, but James didn't need the walls for that—he'd seen it with his own eyes.

He passed by two plinths, one showing a globe, the other a crescent. He thought maybe this meant the moon and the sun, but he wasn't sure what it was supposed to tell him, if anything at all. He barely moved beyond them when his own source of luminance began to wane. The torch flickered a bit, then shone fiercely, then flickered again.

"Come on," he said to it, tapping the side. It was a new battery, so it should've lasted for ages. The light was growing duller in it, and the flickering was increasing, so he felt forced to push ahead a little faster or risk being lost entirely in darkness.

When the torch finally gave up the ghost, he found himself at a crossroads of sorts, barely illuminated by lanterns far down each passage. He thought this might be in some way symbolic of his own uncertainty. He could go left or right, or straight ahead. If it was symbolic, he thought maybe the distractions of either side were best avoided, that he should take the path ahead, unwinding, like an arrow loosed from its bow.

But it wasn't symbolic. It was a trap. As he stepped ahead, he felt the slab beneath his feet sink a little, and he instantly knew that he was in trouble. Yet before he could turn back, the entire ground beneath him gave way, collapsing into a slope, down which he tumbled, bashing his back against the stone.

He clattered off the ground below in a new part of the tomb, which seemed a little better lit than the others. He groaned as he sat up, then forgot his aches when he saw that the flaming lanterns that lined the walls seemed to be extinguishing and lighting again of their own accord. One on either side went out with a flurry of wind, and then the next, and on and on, while two others came back on again. No breeze had the power to do this. It must have been something else.

He sat there for a moment, studying the pattern. It seemed that the first three sets had to go out before the first set of lanterns came back on, leaving a gap of two sets in darkness. This moved on in the same sequence, then seemed to change into an entirely random sequence for two more rounds, before returning to the more predictable order again.

That was all well and good, but he wasn't sure what it meant. He had a hunch it wasn't just decoration, or the sign of bad wiring. The slope behind him was too steep to climb back up, so the only route he could take was straight through the flickering lights. The question was: did he try to stay in the light or the darkness? He mulled this over for a time, until he reckoned it was a question of odds. It wasn't much of a test to stay in the light, because there were far more lanterns on than there were out. It was quite a challenge, however, to hide in the shadows created by the two sets of doused flames, two constantly moving sets, with the fire chasing behind, and blocking the path ahead.

He didn't leave it to chance though. He cast his own extinguished torch into the passage ahead when the lights were on. The torch sizzled and melted away, as if it was the fire of the sun upon it. James could only imagine what it would do to his flesh.

Then, as the lights went out, he made a dash for it, hiding in the shadows, trying not to even let a toe or the tip of his nose enter the beams of light ahead. The next set went out, and he took a step forward into the safety of the shadow, just as the lights flared up behind him. He now felt a little of what the vampires must have felt, hiding in darkness, running from the light.

He continued on, growing more nervous as he did. He only had to slip up once for this to go horribly wrong. The passage seemed infinitely long. Maybe this was also what the vampires felt, living forever.

Eventually he emerged from the trapped corridor into a larger circular chamber, which had some weak lanterns flickering in the centre. They showed what was pressed against the walls: many stone sarcophagi, sealed tightly, with inscriptions marked into them. He tried to read some of them, but they weren't in any language he knew.

Then, just as he pressed his hand against one, the lid moved a little. He jumped back, holding out his hands, even as the stone cracked and fell apart, revealing a vampire, just like Lorcan's father, ancient and terrifying. This one must have been sleeping for a hundred years, but now it was awake, and very hungry.

James circled around the room, holding his hands out, as if that would do any good. The vampire stirred, stepping out slowly in the chamber. It legs shook a little, as if the long sleep had caused some atrophy in them. Perhaps it was more the lack of blood during that long rest. James would make up for it.

They stepped sideways around the room, preparing for the fight, studying each other's movements. James was looking for a weakness, but the vampire was looking for a vein.

Suddenly it leapt at him, and he could not dodge it in time. It pressed him back against another stone coffin, reaching its pointed claws towards his neck. The sarcophagus beneath James then began to shudder and crack. The vampire pulled James away, unwilling to share his meal, just as another ancient vampire emerged.

James backed away from them, almost touching another stone bed, almost waking another of that awful breed. The two vampires snarled at each other, baring their many pointed teeth, brandishing their claws like knives. They sliced through the air in front of them, moving in and pulling back, giving out terrible war cries.

Then they fought, leaping and slashing, one throwing the other, before coming down on it again with a fist of nails. James sidled around the chamber to avoid them both, ducking and dodging, dashing here and stumbling there, until he was knocked back into another coffin. Then a third vampire broke free to join the fight.

There was so little room left to move that James found he was being pushed and pulled back and forth between the vampires, feeling the slice of their claws as they swung for each other, with him in the way. He fell to the ground, kicking his legs at them, then scrambled away just enough to see the lanterns in the hallway he came from. He crawled towards them, but the vampires must have noticed, or sensed his thoughts. All three of them suddenly stopped fighting and turned to him. Then they dashed towards him, even as he crawled faster towards the lights. Just in time, he dove into the darkness, and a set of lights flickered on behind him, straight in the path of the three advancing vampires. All three of them had launched themselves so quickly after him that they ended up throwing themselves straight into the blades of light. They burst into flames with terrible wails, before collapsing into piles of dust.

James followed the pattern of the lights back into the room, careful not to touch any of the other stone coffins, wary also of what was ahead. He limped into the next corridor, slow at first, but eager now to get this over with, to find the way out.

He found himself in a labyrinth, following twisting paths, which often seemed to bring him back to where he started, that same room with five more undisturbed coffins. He tried to map the way in his head, but the place seemed to be playing tricks on his mind. He knew he turned left here, and that brought him round in a circle, so that must be wrong. And yet when he turned right instead, it seemed like the exact same route as before.

Eventually, by luck or fate, he found steps leading down to the next level, but he was dismayed to find another labyrinth there: this time a hall of mirrors, all reflecting each other, showing dozens of him, and not a hint of the way out. They also showed something else, a slab on the ground with the indentations of hands. James wondered if maybe this was a trap, so he leapt over it, smacking his face off a mirror on the other side. Then, as he started to enter the maze, he wondered why a trap would be so clearly labelled, and if maybe instead he was supposed to place his hands in it. Maybe they would recognise a true blood warden and open the way ahead for him.

He went back to the slab and held his hands over it, hoping that he really was a true blood warden, that it didn't have some penalty instead. He pressed his hands into the indentations and waited for something to happen. It didn't seem like anything did. Then he thought he heard something, like moving stone.

He stood up, feeling a slight smile form on his lips. But the sound didn't come from the hall of mirrors, so it wasn't a door opening there. No. It came from back upstairs, from that circular chamber, where the remaining five coffins opened up.

He felt a sudden panic, which propelled him on into the hall of mirrors, feeling his way against the glass. He could hear the vampires snarling upstairs, and knew it wouldn't be long before they found out where he was. For all he knew, they were already in the reflective labyrinth, but no matter how many times they showed himself, those mirrors would never betray the location of the hunting vampires.

He continued on, faster now, feeling his heart pounding, his pulse racing, his breath fleeting. He crashed into mirrors, stubbing his toes, bashing his nose, feeling out for them, and not knowing if maybe he wasn't just going in circles, but was making his way back out to the where the vampires came from, back into their waiting claws.

Then he saw something in the mirrors: a pedestal, with a golden Celtic cross perched upon it. Yet the mirrors were no aid to him, for they showed it in all directions. He might have been close, or he might have been very far away from it.

He felt the presence of the vampires in the maze, so he went even faster than before, charging through, until he no longer saw the pedestal. He turned back, feeling the presence approaching, but knowing he had to go that way, to search for another turn he must have missed before. He found it with one scrambling hand, just as he caught sight of the shimmering cloak of the vampire. That was no reflection. It was here, just within reach.

Then, even as he heard the vampire start to run for

him, he emerged from the hall of mirrors and saw the pedestal ahead. There was the golden cross, similar to the many high crosses that dotted the landscape of Ireland, and which were, according to Mr. Constant, employed as barriers against the vampires and other evil creatures of the land. This gold cross, however, was small enough to be held by hand, and James felt an instant attraction towards it, and a sense of ownership over it, as if he had just stumbled upon a lost toy. Yet this was no toy. It was a weapon.

And he needed a weapon. The vampire came out behind him, snarling.

James ran, feeling the presence charging behind him. The pedestal was just within reach, but he could still die here, stretching his arm out, trying to grasp something, but feeling life slip between his fingers instead.

He arrived at the pedestal, and reached out for the cross. Even as his hand neared it, it started to buzz with energy, and the light around the cross grew suddenly very bright. The creature that was drawing near gave out a fierce cry, and when the light subsided, and James turned with the cross in hand, the creature burst into flames, wailing, until it formed another layer of dust upon the ground.

James stepped down, still clutching the cross, feeling the energy of it travel through him, washing away his doubts, burning away his fears. The weeds of uncertainty were sliced down, and that little seed of strength within him grew suddenly into a great tree of life and light. He knew his calling, his purpose in life, and now felt the blood of the blood wardens pumping through his veins.

THE KISS OF DEATH

The return to Umbra Montis was a jubilant one. James had emerged from the passage tomb changed, and yet unchanged. It wasn't so much a transformation as a realisation of who he always was.

"The Cross is just a symbol of your power," Mr. Constant said. "It has its own energy, true enough, but the real power is in your blood."

"I can feel it," James said. "For the first time, I actually feel alive."

"Well, don't get overconfident," the magician warned. "You can still die yet."

James went with Rua and Caoimh to the old hotel, where Mr. Constant and Lilly said their goodbyes. Lilly would stay with the magician until she found a new place, less for her safety and more for him to keep an eye on her.

The hotel seemed very empty now, more than ever. Rua called out for Lorcan, but there was no response.

"He's probably at the lake," she said.

"Or in it," Caoimh added.

"Get James some new quarters. I have some things to attend to. Now that we have a proven blood warden, that should be the end of all these claims to the thrones. I will start writing the summons to the various families."

She headed off, and Caoimh brought James to one of the larger bedrooms on the top floor, which looked a lot more lavish than the one he had stayed in previously.

"You be good to her," the driver told him.

"What? Me be good to *her*? Should be the other way 'round."

Caoimh sighed, but said nothing more.

James took a bath (he preferred showers, but this place was lucky to even have running water) and got into some fresh clothes. It was odd, but they didn't quite feel like his clothes any more, even though he'd brought them with him from the States. He found a tiny handheld mirror in one of the drawers and used it to shave. Just as he was finished, mopping up a few cuts, he heard a voice.

"You look good."

"Jesus," James said, jumping. He turned to see Rua there, wearing a red lace nightgown.

She tried to stifle a snarl. "You shouldn't use that name."

"Sorry, it's instinct." He paused. "Does that mean the Christians got it right?"

"No. It's just one of many holy names, in many traditions and tongues, that scathes us so." She glanced at the golden Celtic cross on his bed, seeming pained by its presence. "And the cross is just one of many holy symbols of warding. Many others will work just as well."

"And what about mirrors?" James said, holding it up to her. She placed her hand up, as if to block what she thought was an ugly reflection, but there was none. He placed it back on the table, adding: "It's the only mirror you've got in this place."

She tapped the mirror quickly over the edge of the table into the open drawer, which she closed just as quick.

"It's not the *only* one."

"What, the mirror of the soul?"

She cocked her head. "At least we have one between us."

She took his left hand and placed it on her waist, and interlocked her fingers with his other hand. She stared into his eyes, but that hypnotic gaze did not have the same power as it once did. It didn't need to though. James was already entranced.

"Is this not … forbidden?" he asked her.

She drew in close to kiss his neck. "Yes," she whispered. "The forbidden fruit."

"Does that make you the serpent?"

Before he could quite finish the sentence, she kissed him, then bit his lower lip. It was a tender bite, a playful bite, not the snap of the snake.

She pushed him back onto the bed, where he landed on the cross. He pulled it out from beneath him and cast it onto the floor, where its light dulled almost entirely. She crawled onto the bed, and onto him, ripping his shirt open and running her sharp nails down his chest. He pushed her off and rolled around on top of her, pinning her down.

"Turn off the lights," she whispered.

James reached over to the oil lamp and blew out the wick.

"I like the dark," she added.

The room fell into shadow, but the Cross of St. Benedict still gave out a faint glow, just enough to see meeting lips and pressing flesh, just enough to show the silhouette of Lorcan peering through the slightly open door, and just enough for whoever was at the window, taking photographs of that not-so-perfect marriage.

SACRIFICE

They heard Lorcan give out a terrible roar and cast over tables, and tear down bookcases with his telekinetic pull.

"I have given my life to this lie!" he shouted. He continued through the castle, breaking anything in his path.

Rua urged James to leave him be, but James was pushed on by guilt.

"What has he given me?" she asked James as he left the room.

James followed the trail of destruction, finding Lorcan out on the highest ledge of Umbra Montis, his legs dangling over the vast precipice. His right arm leant upon a frowning gargoyle, whose face matched the dour expression upon the vampire's. His left hand held a chain, from which hung a locket.

"You have come to console me," Lorcan said, before James had even drawn near. That superior sense of hearing, and sense of smell, was weakened by the protective powers of a blood warden, but it was still stronger than a normal human.

"Maybe I've come to seek consolement myself," James replied.

He stepped out onto the ledge, catching sight of the sheer drop below, and felt suddenly a little dizzy. The ledge seemed smaller than before, barely big enough to stand on. The gargoyle appeared to be taking up far too much space, and even it clutched the protruding platform with its stone claws.

"You jest," Lorcan said. "What is there that I can aid you with? No. I am no counsellor. You seek not the madman for his wisdom. You seek not the broken for advice on building."

"What are you doing out here?"

"What I have always been doing. Brooding and pining, and trying to take that little extra step towards the edge, towards the end."

"Why do you want it to end?"

Lorcan looked at him with sorrow in his eyes. "Why do you want it to continue?"

"Because I haven't experienced it all."

"Well, I have. Or enough of it to know that I want no more."

"I'm sorry," James said. He wasn't even entirely certain that Lorcan had seen him with Rua, or that he cared. Yet to find him up here on the ledge suggested he cared too much.

"You can have her," Lorcan replied. "Have what I never had. That is what I miss most: love. But love is for the living. I have not seen a drop of it since I became undead. Yet the memory of it lives, perhaps only to taunt and torture me. But what of her? You cannot have her heart if it does not beat. My own?

151

I lie to my ears to make it seem that it still has a rhythm. We are shells, houses for the demons in us. Perhaps when human, we were the same, but at least we shared that house with a soul."

"For a vampire, you kind of sound like you've got a conscience."

"That is perhaps the only thing not yet dead in me. It would be easier if it were buried too, but no! As much as I thirst for blood, I yearn to be free of this curse, and to do some good before I pass." He scoffed. "What passing waits for me? The old may look upon their life and count regrets, and yet may still see those good deeds done, and die happy. For me, the regrets keep counting, and even if I do a deed worthy of honour, I live on to quash it with a dozen deeds of horror."

He moved a stray tile from the roof with his telekinetic powers, grasping it with his hand, before letting it fall down below. There was a clatter as it broke apart on the ground. He looked down on it, and perhaps, if he had some power of foresight, he could see his broken body down there too.

"Do you know what it is like to die every day? It is my eternal torment, my hell on earth. The Devil does not need to come for me, for he resides in me." He tapped the side of his head. "The prodding pitchfork is in my mind. The piercing spear is in my heart. To live without a soul is not to live. You feel always empty. Is is to leave space for the demon to come in."

Lorcan rose suddenly, with a dexterity that dancers would have dreamed of, and a balance envied by acrobats. He seemed well suited to that platform, as much a home to him as it was the stone figure he stood beside.

He stepped forward, closer to the edge. He cast his gaze down to the earth, that global burial mound. His intent was clear.

"Lorcan," James said.

"You are powerful now, James," Lorcan replied, "but you have not the power of the vampire. Your words carry the weight of the living. Mine carry the weight of the dead. Oh, how terrible that weight is. If I could but fix it about my feet, then perhaps I would sink in some ocean, and drown, but instead I float. Gravity is my iron ball, and yet it fails me too."

"Lorcan, don't do this."

"Your worries are wasted. See!"

Suddenly he leapt off the edge, and James ran towards him, reaching out, but caught nothing. He heard the flutter of fabric as the vampire plummeted down, but then it changed to the flapping of wings as Lorcan rose again in a cloud of bats. They flew in place for a moment, staring at James, before they spun in a whisk of shadow into the figure of Lorcan again, standing once more upon the edge. He turned to James with tears in his eyes.

"See!" he repeated, anguished. "The demon in me won't let me die. I leap, but it pulls me up. I fall, but it makes me fly. I do not have the freedom that you do, the freedom to let it all turn to black. I have tried everything. I have bolted myself to an anchor, and cast it and I into the sea, but no chains can hold this demon in me. I have lain upon the tracks, but I stop the train, not my life. I have taken many wooden stakes and driven them towards my heart, that empty vessel, and my hand stops, like a robot, before it pierces my rotten flesh. I have launched myself against the sharpest blades, and set myself beneath the razor of the guillotine, but it has all been to no avail. I have even asked Rua to do it for me, to give me this sweet release, but she refuses. I just want it all to end!"

James was overcome by sympathy for the vampire, or rather that tiny element of humanity in him, buried by the demon. There was no redemption for it, and no freedom. Eternal life was a prison.

It dawned on James then that he could do it, that he could free the vampire from this prison. Yet he knew that just like Lorcan's own attempts, any attack on Lorcan's life would be met with resistance by the demon in him. Lorcan was a formidable vampire, one of an older caste, with powers beyond many, and speed beyond most. It would not be easy.

Lorcan turned and looked at him.

"I know your thoughts," he said.

"It would be asking a lot."

"It would be asking everything."

"I'm not sure I'm strong enough."

Lorcan forced a smile, which was overshadowed by the sadness in his eyes. "I'm not sure you are either. It will fight you. I will fight you, even though I do not will it. Such is the way. We pretend we are kings, but we are pawns. When we are gone, the battle will continue without us."

"The problem is," James said, "we need you for the battle now."

"And there it is," Lorcan replied, "that same

argument that Rua made. She made it a hundred years ago too, and here I am still, still fighting! I'm not sure there is any more fight in me left. I drain people of their blood, of their vitality, and yet I am drained of my will."

"But this is different, right? There hasn't been a war like this in a long time. People depend on us. The world needs us right now. I didn't want this either, Lorcan. You're not the only one who didn't get a choice. Maybe this is bigger than us. Maybe this is how we make a difference. Maybe this is how you make amends."

Lorcan bit his lip. "I am done fighting. I have already made a difference, and it was an evil one. If this empire is to fall, then let it fall! Maybe then I can die in the ashes."

He shifted again into the cloud of bats and flew off into the night sky. Where he went, no one knew. Perhaps he tried, as he so often did, to help some poor living soul, a token effort to appease his not yet rotten conscience. And perhaps, as equally often, the demon in him took that poor living soul and made it into a meal.

TOO MANY FANGS

The Gorman family never got Rua's summons. They were out on the road, close to Ballyboden, where it seemed there was a lot more activity than there should have been.

"I don't like the looks of it," John Gorman said.

"I can scout," his son, Frankie, responded. He was just twelve years old when he was turned, and that had only been less than a year ago. He'd stay that age forever, even if he lived a thousand years. Normally it was forbidden to turn a child, but John Gorman risked everything to save Frankie from a life-threatening illness. He even risked his soul.

"G'wan then," John said.

He knew there was no one faster than Frankie on his feet. They parked on the road, far enough away from the O'Neill stronghold to stay out of sight, but close enough in case of an emergency. They didn't know how close to war they were.

Frankie sneaked up to one of the lower walls and peeked over, straining on the tips of his toes. What he witnessed almost knocked him from his feet. There, down in the circular chamber, were dozens of people, all being turned, several at a time, into vampires.

It was a violation of the blood quota enforced by the government, the only reason they let the vampires continue to operate in the country without resistance. So long as they kept their numbers down, and the number of meals down too, the people in power would turn a blind eye. But the O'Neills were making an army. There was no way you could ignore this.

Frankie watched as Dearg marched through the formations, shouting orders, sending her kin to go out and drag more hapless humans into the chamber. She hauled some of the new vampires up, charging them to give an oath of allegiance to her and the family name. They obeyed, swearing even to die for her. They'd already done it once.

Then one of the vampires looked up, spotting Frankie. The boy dived down, pressing his back against the wall, panting. If he were still human, he would have hoped that he hadn't been seen. But he was a vampire himself, so he knew with grim certainty that they had spied him.

It took a moment for the flood of panic to wash away, before his instinct to hide became an instinct to run. He dashed away from the wall, just as two dozen vampires climbed over it and gave chase.

Frankie raced through the dirt paths, leaping over the gnarled roots of trees, splashing through puddles, part-tripping, part-stumbling. He could feel the hunters gaining on him, especially the true

O'Neills. He could almost feel their razor-sharp nails slicing through his neck.

One of the vampires leapt at him, swiping at the back of his right leg. It tore a gash in his trousers, and a strip of flesh from his calf. He yelped and faltered, and only the fear of annihilation spurred him on. He limped forward, dragging his wounded limb behind, finding it harder to jump now, and harder to dive and dash away.

Then another vampire came, snarling and slashing, shredding the back of Frankie's jacket, leaving a trail of blood dripping down him. The force of the attack sent Frankie tumbling forward and down a mound lined with soggy leaves. He clambered to his feet, disorientated, catching sight of the approaching silhouettes, which flittered through the trees behind him.

Then he ran again, out now into the road, his pace slowed, his steps awkward. He advanced a bit, then collapsed down, before pushing himself back up to take another few steps away. He knew he was done for, but he defied that knowledge, searching for some extra seconds of life.

As the hunters came out of the forest, watching Frankie bob and weave, and rise and fall, Frankie spotted the two wagons up ahead, and his own people crowded around them.

"Gather!" he shouted, reverting to the tongue of his people.

John peered out of the second wagon, which was a few metres further down the road on the right. His eyes widened at the sight of his son stumbling towards him, and a tsunami of vampires coming down behind. It seemed for a moment that he was about to come out to fight, but then he saw Dearg appear behind the wall of newly-made vampires, and the Brute Brothers with her.

"Awást!" John cried in Gammon to the driver.

As many of the Gorman family as possible bundled into the wagon, just as the driver set about whipping the horses into a light trot. Frankie raced past the first wagon, where the people were slower to get on board. The vampires struck that one like a flood, crashing through the wood, slashing and slicing. The Gormans there fought back fiercely, beating some of the newly-turned vampires to a bloody pulp. But there were too many of them, and soon the O'Neills were there, slaughtering the few remaining Gormans in that wagon.

Frankie continued his retreat, finding it harder to catch up with the second wagon, which was now moving steadily away.

"Run, kan!" his father shouted, stretching out his hand towards him. The tips of their fingers grazed each other, but then the horses picked up speed, and Frankie fell behind again.

Frankie couldn't see it, but he knew the look of desperation on his own face was harrowing. He was already starting to feel like giving up, that he couldn't make it to the wagon in time. A few of the vampires had broken off from the first wagon to pursue him.

"Slow it down!" his father told the driver.

The wagon slowed, and Frankie gave it one last effort. He put everything into that run, just as the vampires behind were closing in again. His father reached out once more, and now he gripped the boy's hand, and pulled him into the wagon, both of them falling to the floor in a mix of relief and pain.

The driver lashed the horses, and now they galloped. The vampires fell behind, turning back to the first wagon, where there was a mighty feast of blood and flesh.

"You're safe, kan," John told his son, resting a hand upon the boy's shoulder.

But Frankie could see through the curtain at the back, where the first wagon, now driven by the O'Neills, was starting up. The horses were slain and bled dry, but Dearg worked a different set of reins, pulling the astral strings that set the wheels in motion.

Frankie was safe for now, but the Gormans still had a long road to ride, and the most vicious vampire clan hot on their heels.

THE WAGON CHASE

The wagons bounded down the uneven road, turning corners sharply, sending up muck behind them and causing a tremendous din as the horses galloped and the wheels span with a frenzy. The first wagon, in which the surviving Gormans sat, was fast, but the second wagon, with Dearg's spellcasting, was gaining on them.

"We won't last long at this rate," John said.

"We shoulda fought 'em!" Pat 'Bruiser' Gorman replied.

"We'll fight 'em yet. But not off guard. It isn't a fair fight."

"Those O'Neills never fight fair."

"We've too much weight," Frankie's older cousin, Mary, shouted. "I'll take my lot south."

Before John could stop her, Mary leapt off the wagon with her son and daughter, the three of them charging into the safety of the trees. As the O'Neill wagon passed, a handful of vampires hopped off to chase them.

With fewer people onboard, the first vehicle

picked up speed. But speed alone would not be enough, not with Dearg in pursuit.

The wagon rocked suddenly, and something blasted a hole through the canopy.

"What was that?" Pat asked.

"That'll be the Red Hag," John replied. "She's the reason there isn't no fair fights here."

He pulled back the curtain at the back of the wagon, where they could see Dearg standing at the front of the other wagon, hanging out of the door, casting small bolts from her hands towards them. John ducked as one flew by his head.

"Nan," he called.

Out of the front, sitting with the driver, came Nan Gorman, the matriarch of the family. She wasn't a vampire, and they never turned her, respecting her wishes, but she stayed with them all the same. It was just as well, because she was the only one of them who knew anything about magic.

Nan hobbled into the back, clutching a pile of talismans strung together. They didn't ward off vampires, or she'd have no family at all. They stored some of the power she had amassed over the years, like a battery. Now it was time to spend it.

"Get outta me way!" she growled at Pat and John as she came through. She had never quite forgiven them for getting involved in this dark side of the world, or for bringing Frankie with them. But you didn't get to pick your family, living or dead.

Nan grabbed a handle at the back of the wagon, holding out her talismans in the other. She swung her head through the curtain to get a better look, and pulled it back in time as Dearg fired another bolt her way.

"That witch!" Nan said. Some said that about her too, but she'd slap you if you called it witchcraft. This was good solid Christian magic, as far as she was concerned. That some of her family weren't quite in the state to be good solid Christians any more was beside the point.

She shook the talismans and pointed her hand through the curtain. A bolt of electricity extended from it to the other wagon, and Dearg retreated inside. Then she edged out again, returning fire. Nan did the same, until both of them were lashing bolts left and right, tearing up parts of the road, and leaving sizzling marks upon the sides of the wagons.

Then a bolt struck one of the back wheels of the first vehicle, splintering the wood. The wagon slumped down and slowed, and the horses found it difficult to pull. Another bolt came, destroying the wheel entirely.

Nan came back inside, shaking her head, and seeming like she would slap anyone who said anything to her. She hustled past John and sat down beside Frankie, casting at him the only look of sympathy she had in her. She held the talismans in both hands, then closed her eyes. After a brief moment, she began rotating her hands in circles, and outside formed a spectral wheel where the other one was missing. She kept spinning, and now it span in turn, and the wagon sped to life again.

The chase continued, but now Nan Gorman had to divide her attention between the wheel, which she kept going with her right hand, and the other wagon, which she attacked with her left. She raised her left hand high, palm outwards, and formed a shield around them, then pressed the shield outwards, until it struck the other vehicle, slowing it down. This was more tiring than all the other efforts, but it was also the most effective, so she did it again.

Yet to poor Frankie, who peeked outside, it seemed that Dearg had stopped her now fruitless attacks and had gone back behind the curtain. He didn't know much about magic, but he'd heard enough of Nan's tales to know that Dearg didn't give up easily. If she was silent now, she wasn't still. She'd be working on something else, something big.

The gap between the wagons grew, but the horses were growing tired, and the driver warned that they could only keep up this pace for so long. They only hoped that Dearg too was tiring, that she didn't have access to that infinite well of magic that some said she did.

"We're out of their reach!" John declared, smiling.

Frankie peered out and saw the other wagon fading into the blackness of the night far behind. It seemed like a good sign, but he couldn't help but feel in the pit of his stomach that it was a bad omen. Nan must've felt it too, because she came back in with a grim look upon her face.

Suddenly there was a flash of light, like far-off lightning, and Dearg's wagon seemed to appear out of nowhere side-by-side with their own. With just as much speed, vampires leapt from the doorways of that one to the next, clutching the side of the Gormans' wagon, sidling along or climbing onto the roof.

"I guess we fight now," Bruiser said, showing his fists.

"I guess we die now," John said. He was never much of a fighter.

Nan rose to her feet, firing a wall of energy at one of the vampires that came through the curtain at the back. She readied for the next, while the others stood back-to-back, fangs bared, fists raised.

They heard the thuds and stomps of vampires on the roof, and the whacks against the walls when several more jumped across. There were too many of them. The Gormans could fight, but they knew that sooner or later—and likely very soon—they would lose.

"Don't let them turn me," Nan pleaded. That was what she'd made John and Pat promise her before. They let her age gracefully, let her keep her soul, and keep her place in heaven. That was what she feared the most. She still wore a crucifix around her neck, but it was tiny, out of love for her sons.

John and Pat said nothing. Frankie knew they'd try their best, that they'd go to the ends of the earth—and beyond—for family, just like they had for him. He was only alive, if this was life, because of them. He didn't even have to hunt for blood like they did. They did it for him, spared him the horror of the slaughter. He was still newly turned, less than a year, almost as fresh as the O'Neill's entire army. He thought he'd live at this age forever. He never thought it'd end so soon.

The vampires crawled inside.

Then both wagons halted suddenly.

Up ahead, the road was blocked by three more wagons, but these ones were different in style, with Gothic elements in their design. There were hundreds of metal and wooden crosses nailed across their hulls. Standing before them were several dozen people, so-called "gypsy" folk, wearing black, with metal masks, all adorned with hundreds more smaller crosses. You couldn't see any of their faces. The masks were made up of hundreds of large nails.

Inside the Gormans' wagon, the vampires froze in place.

"Who the hell are they?" one of them asked.

Nan knew the answer. It brought some comfort, but also some pain. "The Order of Nails," she said, knowing that her family were at as much risk of them as the O'Neills' new recruits were.

THE ORDER OF NAILS

They called themselves Strigoi Stalkers, and they were members of the Order of Nails. Their identity was secret, and though the Order had originated as a Romani gypsy group, it now included members of various backgrounds—all united by the desire to wipe out the vampire scourge.

They leapt into action, charging towards the vampires with weapons bared. At the back, more Stalkers stood, firing crossbows full of nails, which were dipped in holy water. Their aim was not just to eradicate, but to inflict as much suffering as possible to those evil fiends.

Their leader, Manus, stood out easily, for his helm was adorned on the top with a large metal cross the size of his head. It must have been heavy, and unwieldy, but he wore it with ease. He carried a giant flail, the head of which was encrusted with hundreds of outward-pointing nails. When he swung it, it caught in the flesh of a vampire, and he pulled them close to finish them off.

Several Stalkers caught fleeing vampires and held

them down. The vampires squirmed and screamed, for even the gloves of the Stalkers had nails and crosses on them. Yet all of that was nothing compared to what the vampires faced now.

Manus approached the first of them and knelt down nearby. He took a long, thick, rusty nail from his belt, said to have been used to affix Christ to the cross, and lined it up at the forehead of the vampire. Then he took a hammer from his belt and held it aloft.

"Through this we cleanse even Hell itself," he said, his voice muffled by the mask, and made to sound a lot more sinister.

Another Stalker came by, holding a glass cube towards the crown of the vampire's head. Inside the cube, the walls were lined with many more little nails, all doused in holy water or anointed oil. There was something else in it that no one ever spoke of, but could attract demons like fish to bait.

The vampire seemed about to say something, but the leader of the Order of Nails drove the hammer home, and so the nail pierced through the head of the creature. Another tap and it went in further, eliciting another blood-curdling scream.

A black smoke rose from the wound, growing in size, and the Cube-holder trapped it inside the glass vessel, where it visibly writhed in pain. She brought it back to one of the wagons, where there were dozens more cubes with their own shadowy victims, all facing eternal torment. These were only the ones recently collected. There were far more in the hidden dungeons of the Order of Nails, going back a century, to the time when the blood wardens abandoned their watch.

Inside the first wagon, there was no fight. The O'Neill army fled, or fought with the Stalkers, until the ground outside was littered with dust.

"Stay in here if you know what's good for ya," Nan warned her family. There was a troubled look in her eyes, more troubled even than when they came to her with news of their plans to turn the sick and feeble Frankie in one last-ditch effort to save his life.

Nan hobbled outside, casting a few paltry magical bolts at the fleeing vampires, not to hurt them, but to demonstrate to the Order of Nails that they were her enemy too.

Manus approached. He looked at the cross around her neck, tiny though it was.

"A fellow believer," he said.

"Till the day I die," she replied.

"Not today then."

They stared at each other for a moment.

"We were attacked on the road," Nan explained. That wasn't a lie, so it was easier to say.

"You are lucky," Manus said, "that the road is stalked by good as well as evil."

"Yes."

"Why did they want you?"

"God knows why."

"Yes," he said, his voice suddenly deep and rumbling, like thunder. "He does."

"Blood, I guess."

"That was quite a force for a little feast. How many of you are there?"

"There's only a handful of us left. We numbered a few dozen at first. Most were in the other wagon. It was what slowed 'em down."

"My sympathies."

Nan hung her head. Those were good people, and not all of them were vampires. The Gormans stuck together, living or dead. They had a saying: "You travel the long road with kin, an' travel the longer roads after with 'em too."

"Well," the leader said. "Let a fellow gypsy go back to the road now safely. The way ahead is clear, for we have cleared it. The way back … we'll clear that too."

She nodded to them and walked back to the wagon.

"And be careful," he told her as she neared the door. "Evil has a way of getting close. You never know where you might find it."

She sighed as she climbed inside and looked at her vampire kin.

THE MONOLITH

On that same night, James met up with Lilly in the City Centre, finally getting some time to catch up after all the trouble of the past few days. They went to an old pub around the corner from Trinity College, pretty much at the heart of the city, and yet tucked away enough that few people really knew about it. Those who did tended to avoid it too.

Inside, it was dim, cosy, and quaint. It had been refurbished over the years, but some of the original style and furnishings remained, and what was new was deliberately weathered. The walls in some parts were lined with old newspapers, and the central area had a gigantic wooden face as a fireplace, with the gaping mouth leading to the logs and flames. That fire seemed to be always on, night and day.

The pub was called the Monolith, and it was run by Oscar Elsey, a burly effeminate man, who looked at times like he was deciding between hugging you and knocking your lights out. James was glad that Oscar seemed to like Lilly. He ran to her and picked her up in his muscly arms.

"Girl, you are looking *fine*," he said in his shrill voice.

They exchanged some moment of glee, hopping up and down together, until Oscar noticed James and became suddenly very butch, then just as suddenly very camp again.

"*Umm-hmm*. Girl, what sorta wolf did you catch?"

Lilly beamed. "This is James."

"The blood warden?"

"That's the one."

James offered his hand, and Oscar grasped it with both of his. He had a fierce grip. "Forgive me if I howl," he said, "but boy, you're a specimen all right." He held James' jaw for a moment, feeling the square edges. Then he turned and led them off, shouting back, "*Umm!*"

They followed him through the mouth of the fireplace, where the flames vanished just seconds before they passed, and came back on just as quickly. This was the rumoured "back room," which normal patrons of the bar didn't get to see. When James glanced around, he could see why. The place was filled will all sorts of the weird and wonderful: witches, vampires, werewolves, fey, ghosts, even a necromancer with a party of zombies.

Oscar brought Lilly aside, leaving James at the bar.

"Eh, something with no blood in it," he said. "Like a beer or something."

"And no eyes too, I suppose," the barman said. He didn't smile, so James wasn't entirely sure he was joking.

"No. No eyes, please."

James stared for a moment as the barman poured him a beer. "So, what are you?"

"I'm the barman."

"Yeah, but … like, are you an alien or a robot or a creature from another dimension, or what?"

"I'm … just the barman."

"Human?"

"Uh, yes."

"Oh."

They stared at each other for a moment.

"Sorry. It's just … you know." James gestured around the room, and realised he probably shouldn't be drawing attention to himself.

"What are you?" the barman asked.

James smiled. "You know, I don't quite know yet."

Someone tapped him on the shoulder. "I do. You're in a world of trouble." James turned to see Ioana Danesti standing there, her face as dour and stern as ever. She held up a photo to him, which showed him in bed with Rua. "This has been sent to all the families. Everyone knows. You can tell Rua that her summons will go unanswered. Having a blood warden on her side is one thing. Having it in her bed is another. The perfect marriage is over. You'll get no support from us in the war ahead."

HOUSE HOOLIGAN

They came from Millwall, London, and they called themselves the Favoured Fangs. They weren't the favourites of anyone who met them. They caused havoc throughout Britain, but Ireland remained largely outside their sphere of influence, thanks to the strong control of the Kavanagh clan. With that crumbling by the second, the Fangs came out and crossed the Irish Sea.

They came by boat, and operated their own ships. They brought crates of supplies with them, the kind that don't get through customs. But these vampires got through no problem. They battered the guards to death with their baseball bats. And they loved it. They loved it almost more than blood.

"Right, you lot!" the leader, Boxer, said. He liked the crack of a baseball bat as much as the rest of them, but what he really loved was bare-knuckle boxing. It usually ending with a few dozens strikes to a bloodied face. Sometimes it didn't end at all until he was dragged away.

"The so-called Kavanagh empire's fallin'," he

continued, spitting that foul family name out of his mouth. "We're not 'ere to claim the thrones. We're 'ere to 'ave a right good laugh about it all, and get the Kavs laughin' too. Let's give 'em all bloody smiles, and let's show 'em that no one, not no Irish or Romanian or anything, can tell us where we can an' cannot go!"

There was a chorus of hoarse and chesty cheers, and an almost rehearsed routine of bats patting hands. Those smooth ones were if you got lucky. They had ones with nails and studs as well.

ALL ROADS LEAD TO
UMBRA MONTIS

James raced back to Umbra Montis, where a crowd was already gathering. He could see the banners of the O'Connor family, which were a sizeable number, as they paraded about in front of the building, chanting and shouting. It almost looked like a kind of protest, but James knew it would not be long before it was a battle.

He sneaked in through the back, rushing upstairs to where he found Rua standing on the highest balcony with John Gorman, surveying the forces below.

"I know," she said, before James fully drew up beside her.

James panted from the race up the steps. Before he fully caught his breath, he could see the amassing armies in the shadow-swept fields. He felt a little bit like watching the beginnings of a siege. Except that there was barely anyone in the castle.

"Was it them?" he asked. "The O'Neills, I mean."

"Of course it was them!" John growled. "They're behind everything. They attacked my family on the road. They've been breeding like rabbits in that hole of theirs."

"It doesn't matter who it was," Rua said, sounding resigned. "It matters who fights."

"Well, the Danestis won't," James told her.

"No," she said softly. "Not even Lorcan. He hasn't been back yet."

"So, who can we count on?" James asked.

Rua turned to John with pleading eyes.

"I'm sorry, Rua," John said, "but I can't risk losing more of my family. I can't even justify them coming to your aid. You broke the sacred tradition that has kept all our families at peace." He turned to James. "You were supposed to be the peace-keeper, not the bringer of war."

Rua looked at him, taking his hand. "It was only a matter of time, John."

He yanked his hand free. "Save your devilry for the next man." He stormed off, leaving Rua alone with James.

"Just us," James said. "That's kind of what got us into this mess."

She turned to him, but did not take his hand. She knew where loneliness had guided her, and what doom it had wrought upon them. She had locked up her heart for the good of the vampire kingdoms, and the safety of humans too. By unlocking it, she had also unleashed many horrors. "This mess" was the understatement of a century.

"Just us," she repeated. "That's what'll get us out

of it as well."

PARTY CRASHING

The stage was set for war, but fate had a cruel way of working things. The O'Connor clan grew in number, waiting to bolster their forces even more before their assault, or maybe just hoping the show of size would make the Kavanaghs give up the thrones willingly. But something else happened. A limousine pulled up, followed by two other cars, and out stepped the most unlikely soldiers. They kind of looked like the guests of a hen party.

James raced downstairs to bring them in before the O'Connors got to them. They stumbled in, half-drunk already, and between their giggles they could be heard saying all sorts of things, like "I wonder if it's haunted" or "I love what you did with the banners outside. Very medieval."

"It's a bad time," James told them.

One of the women hobbled over to him, grabbing him by the collar with one hand and holding out a half-empty bottle of wine with the other. "No such thing, love."

Another woman blew a party horn in his ear,

and the assembly of nine woman half-marched, half-tripped their way up the stairs, screaming and shouting, and doing what they thought was dancing.

"What are they doing here?" Rua asked from the top of the stairs.

James shrugged. He glanced at the bookings at the counter in the foyer. "Looks like Ebed has them down for tonight and tomorrow."

One of the women passed Rua, turning to her. "I'm getting married!" She dashed up the steps.

Another woman stopped where Rua stood and looked her up and down. "Here, Laura!" she shouted up at the bride. "Why can't we have dresses like, hic, this?" She pawed at the silk of Rua's gown.

James grimaced, barely finishing the expression before Rua, still looking down at him, gave a slight push of her hand, which threw the bridesmaid up the full flight of stairs. The woman screamed, and the entire brood of hens screamed too, racing away in all directions, barricading themselves in some of the empty rooms.

Rua shook her head. "We need to get them out of here."

At that moment, James heard more cars pulling up outside. "God, not more of them."

Rua sighed, and James felt something communicated by her breath. This wasn't more unexpected guests, though they were unwelcome ones. This was the O'Neills.

"You better get your cross," Rua told him. "We now have two armies to fight."

* * *

Several black cars pulled up outside, followed by a truck. The doors opened one by one, and out came Dearg and her kin. The truck was packed with dozens of newly-minted vampires, enough to rival the force of the O'Neills, and all eager to prove their worth.

"Nice flag," Dearg shouted over to Cathal O'Connor. She raised her hand, and, with a twist and flourish, she called down a bolt of lightning, which struck the banner he carried, setting it ablaze. He growled at her, but backed away when the Brute Brothers drew up behind her.

They marched up to the front door and kicked it in. Dearg cast Ebed's head through the opening. "Brought you back something," she yelled.

There was no response. Dearg swaggered in, with a dozen vampires behind her, stopping at the end of the stairs. "Hello?" she shouted, her voice echoing through the giant hall.

She turned around, arms outstretched, and looked up as she spun. There, at the top of the highest stairs, she saw Rua, her claws digging deep into the bannisters.

"Come down, Miss Maj," Dearg shouted up. "Come down off your false throne. It's time to play."

But just as quickly as Rua appeared, she vanished out of view.

Dearg smiled, showing her fangs. "Looks like we're playing hide and seek."

BATTLE OF THE BRUTES

James retreated to his room, finding the shaking bride there. She had found the cross and held it up at him as if it might ward him off.

"Give me that," he said as he reefed it off her.

As he walked to the door, he turned and looked at her trembling form. "Hide."

Before he'd even finished the word, and before the bride let out a terrible scream, a fist punched through the door and seized James, hauling him out into the corridor in a haze of splinters. The hand belonged to Paddy O'Neill, one of the Brute Brothers, and the other bounded up the hallway to join them.

James freed himself from the giant's grasp and backed away, but he did not run. The twins towered over him liked they always did, but now he wasn't as intimidated by their bulking forms or their enormous shadows. He stood, defiant, holding the Cross of St. Benedict aloft, where it radiated a subtle light.

"I'm not afraid of no cross!" Joe O'Neill growled, stomping forward.

True enough, he didn't baulk at the sight of that

holy symbol, but as soon as he came within range, James swung the cross, striking the giant, and sending him flying into the wall, as if their roles had suddenly reversed.

Paddy's eyes widened. Not in a hundred years had he seen such power wielded by a mortal, strong enough to knock his twin aside. He hesitated, like James might have done if he did not feel this well of power coursing through his veins, those same veins the O'Neills could not puncture without facing terrible consequences.

Joe clambered up from the fractured ruins of the wall, casting aside brick and plaster, groaning as he got to his knees. He looked at this twin in anger, astonished that he was just standing there. It was only when he got to his feet that Paddy raced in to join him.

James struck Paddy aside, tearing apart the outer wall. The window smashed, and Paddy almost tumbled out. The moonlight streamed in, but it was the light of the cross that illuminated the corridor much more brightly.

Joe caught the cross between both his hands as James tried a backhand strike against him. Yet, though the giant managed to halt the attack, his hands blistered and burned, as if the metal of the cross were the base of a heated prying pain. He screamed, then let go, and stumbled backwards of his own accord, tripping up over the ruins he had just emerged from.

With how easy he had flicked the two away like flies, James started to grow a little overconfident, and a little careless. The next time they came, they came together from either side, and James was not able to switch from one to the other before a massive fist struck him in the jaw. He fell back, crashing onto the floor. The cross leapt from his clutch and clattered off the marble far behind. The wind was knocked from him, and he gasped for breath.

Then the twins stood over him, smiling. James tried to turn and grab the cross, but it was several metres out of reach. Joe grabbed him and pulled him away, throwing him back across to the other side of the hall. The force of the grip was only matched by the pounding of the floor.

James felt a trickle of liquid down his chin. His lip was busted. The twins' eyes grew a little manic at the sight and smell of the blood. Whatever strength they already had would now be multiplied by their bloodlust.

James got to his unsteady feet, breathing heavy, holding out his hands before him, not sure how he could ward off blows, or punch back with enough force to match the cross. He saw it glinting far off down the corridor, well out of reach.

Then the twins came for him.

And he ran for them.

Just as they were about to crash, like a rodent diving against a brick wall, he dropped to the floor and skidded between the legs of Paddy. He half-crawled, half ran, stretching out towards the cross, until his fingers grazed the surface of it.

Then Joe seized him by the ankles and pulled him back a bit. Paddy stepped with his massive boot on James' spine. The blood warden cried out as he felt the bones crushing. It seemed like it all was over. They would add him to the trophy cabinet.

Then a presence appeared far down the corridor, out on the balcony. Everyone looked in that direction simultaneously, feeling that tremendous power. The balcony doors blew open with a gust of wind, and a flurry of bats span and twisted into the form of a man: Lorcan. He raised his head, and his eyes were a terrifying red. Then he raised his hands, and the cross rose too. He pushed them forward, and it flew forward, all the while with Lorcan's hands burning from the astral touch.

The cross came within reach of James' outstretched hand. He grabbed it, and Joe backed away, but Paddy stayed there, keeping James pinned to the ground with his foot.

Then Lorcan advanced down the corridor. Joe started to run, but Paddy stood his ground. Lorcan held his hands out again, and seemed strained, as if lifting a terrible weight. Paddy rose a little, and then with a flick of Lorcan's wrists, the vampire king pressed the giant against the ceiling.

James clambered up, groaning from the pain in his back. Lorcan could not hold the weight, and let Paddy drop to the ground with a crash.

"Slay him!" Lorcan bellowed.

James leapt upon Paddy, holding up the cross. The end of it turned suddenly sharp, like a stake. Paddy tried to punch and swat, but Lorcan used his telekinetic abilities to pin the Brute's arms to his sides, forming his own shape of a cross.

"To Hell with you!" Lorcan said.

James drove the golden stake into Paddy's chest. The vampire spasmed, coughing up a spew of what looked like coal and lava. He burned, and then turned to dust.

James stood up, exhausted. "Good of you to lend a hand."

"Two," Lorcan said, showing his own burnt paws. "And there's nothing good about me at all. But there's nothing good about them either. Less of us in the world, well, *that's* a good thing!"

THE SILENT SISTER

L orcan flew back outside to join the mounting battle, roaming through the black fields like a battering ram, knocking down wave after wave of vampires from the O'Connor clan, the O'Neill family, or the Favoured Fangs, the latter of which arrived in bulk, pouring into the castle to swing their bats and clubs at everything in sight.

Inside, James followed suit, forging a path through the O'Neill army, staking vampire after vampire, coating the floors in a thick layer of dust. Some of the newer and weaker creatures of the night barely even got in reach of him before they exploded from the painful push of the cross.

Yet, though James whittled down their numbers with ease, there was another, stronger vampire making her slow pursuit. No one was entirely sure of her real name, or if she was even related to Dearg. They called her the Silent Sister, for she never spoke, and barely made any sounds at all. Some said that she had a dispute with her elder sister, and Dearg tore her tongue out as a lesson. Yet, for all this, the Silent

Sister maintained a certain unbreakable loyalty, the kind of loyalty that meant breaking others.

The way ahead was clear, but James was wary. He tip-toed down the corridor, cross raised high, ready to strike at a moment's notice. He knew too well, however, that he'd get no notice at all. His eyes searched out every shifting shadow, every flicker of candlelight. His nose hunted the scent of the dead, though he knew they could mask that too. Most of all he relied on his gut, on his instincts, and that told him to be careful, that danger wasn't just around the corner—it was all around him.

He halted suddenly, feeling a presence, though it seemed distant. He turned slowly, seeing nothing down the corridor. He paused for a moment, waiting for the strike, but nothing came. Then he returned to the path ahead, taking a few paces forward before stopping and turning again. Yet nothing happened then either.

Then, as he turned back, keeping his eyes on the door ahead, something emerged from around the corner far behind him: the Silent Sister. She stood for a moment, arms drooping, head lolling to one side, as if she had been hanged, and was still swinging. Then she opened her mouth, as if to scream, but no sound came. Instead, she started to fade away, changing into a gaseous form, so thin and faint that it could barely be seen up close, never mind far away.

James swung around, holding the cross before him. But he saw nothing, even though the Silent Sister was there, drifting slowly towards him. The walls saw. The floor saw. The ceiling saw. Yet just as the Silent Sister was dumb, James was blind.

James stared down the corridor, feeling something, but seeing nothing but the silent walls, the unspeaking curtains, the untouched carpets. For the Silent Sister did not walk towards him. She floated through the air unseen. He looked right through her, but she saw him.

He gave a brief sigh and shook his head. Then he turned back to his original path and took a step forward. It almost felt like something took a step behind him, but that couldn't be. He advanced again, and that same feeling came upon him.

Then with a swiftness like a sudden gale, the gaseous form came around him and became solid in an instant. And there she was, the Silent Sister, pressed against his back, her left arm around his torso, her right hand, clutching a long knife, thrust towards his neck.

His breath was caught, and the shock of it almost made him drop the cross. She held him close, so tight that he could not seem to get the air back into his lungs. The blade pressed deep, nicking his skin, and she might have licked the blood if it weren't poison to her. Instead, she leant in close to him, opening her tongueless mouth right next to his left ear. Maybe she roared. Maybe she screamed. And maybe in his soul he heard her.

Though the press of the blade against his neck made him try to clutch it, made him focus on the squeezing of his throat, he fought his instincts and turned his attention to the cross. Not only did this give him strength; it gave him wisdom. He put his hand down, pressing the ancient talisman against the Silent Sister's leg, where it sizzled.

She turned suddenly to gas again, freeing him from the bladed noose. He swung around to find her, but she appeared solid again behind him, still brandishing the knife. He felt her appear, and so he dived forward just in time as she stabbed the air where he had been. He rolled on the floor, turning on the spot and holding out the cross in front of him. But she was invisible again.

There was no winning this fight so long as she continued to go in and out of visible form, shifting around him, sending him spinning. He thrust the cross out randomly, but it struck nothing, and she dodged it and him with ease. He found it much more difficult to evade her attacks, for she swung at him as she was materialising, cutting him on the arm, then the back, then the chest. She didn't have to suck his blood to bleed him dry.

So he looked to the cross again for wisdom, and it told him to stop, so he stopped. This must have put the Silent Sister on guard, for she halted her attacks too, wary. Then he closed his eyes, immersing himself in darkness. It almost seemed like suicide, like he was giving up, but once he let go of his fear of the situation, he started to see. In the blackness of his closed eyelids, he saw the flickers of something ahead. It was her. She couldn't hide from him now.

Suddenly she darted towards him, but he held the cross towards her, and she recoiled. Then she swept around him, but he turned with her, blocking her next attack, and fending off another. She couldn't sigh or shout, or make any audible expression of her frustration, but he felt it from her.

Then, as she disappeared once more and was in the process of re-emerging behind him, he turned with a speed to match her own and stabbed the now-pointed end of the cross into the air. Her body formed around it. Her heart materialised in the path of the golden stake. She opened her mouth to gasp, but nothing came. Then she made her final shifting form as she tumbled to the ground in a pile of dust.

MIRROR, MIRROR

Dearg pursued Rua through the castle, using magic to chase her scent. She followed her up to the highest level, and then back down again on the far side of the building, through the dimmest hallways, into the cobweb-laced chambers.

She found Caoimh along the path, trying to fend her off with a large spear. She laughed at his attempt, even though she admired his dedication to his family. At least he'd die an honourable death.

He thrust at her, but she simply stepped out of the way and grabbed the metal shaft. "Hold on tight," she said, before a blast of electricity came from her hand, straight through the spear, into Caoimh. He smouldered, unable even to scream, before collapsing into a pile of ash upon the floor.

She stepped forward, planking a boot into his remains, leaving her print. She continued on her hunt for Rua, letting the dust trail along behind her.

The scent of the vampire queen seemed to end in the old gala hall, a huge, long room with a high ceiling, from which hung many giant chandeliers.

It was lavish once, but now it was dark, and the furniture was covered with sheets, dust and cobwebs. The lighting was dim, like much of the hotel, but in this room it was multiplied in the reflections cast by a colossal mirror which ran from one end of the room to the other.

Dearg stalked her way through the furniture placed like obstacles. When she emerged from behind an old cupboard, she cast an illusory shadow in the mirror. At times, she used her magic to help her blend in with humans, to go undetected, to wreak havoc from inside. Now, she used it to strengthen her. The shadow she cast was no mere reflection. It was magnified. As she walked, wisps of shadow swept behind her in the mirror, and the ground seemed to quake in the glass.

She continued on through the slithering path, and in the mirror other things followed. She called them her pets, but some of them were slaves. They were dark things, shadows and spectres. In the real world, they could not be seen. In this mirror, they showed some form.

Finally, she emerged into an open stretch of the hall, and stood face to face with Rua, just feet apart. She hunched over, arms curved, legs bent, rocking back and forth, and side to side. Rua stood perfectly straight and still, thin and shapely, the elbow of her right arm resting on the wrist of her left, as if she were indeed at a ballroom, holding a glass of wine, or blood, in her hand. She cast no reflection in the mirror.

"Mirrors, huh?" Dearg asked.

Rua gave a flicker of a smile, like the spark that lights a fuse.

"You always did like a spectacle," Dearg continued. "Don't think that wasn't another reason why they liked you."

"Why they *like* me," Rua corrected.

"I'm speaking past tense. Getting used to it. You know, for the future."

"Then you better speak all you need to say now. For the future."

Dearg charged at Rua, shouting out her war-cry. Her advance was so swift and frightening, and her look so manic, and her shout so fierce, that most would have baulked before her, and fled. But Rua stood like stone, and when the tide of Dearg came upon her, she merely flicked her wrist and arm ever so slightly, and swatted Dearg away like a fly. Dearg flew across the room, her tangled shadowy form in the mirror showing all the agony that she felt, and crashed into one of the covered bookcases, sending a tumble of dusty tomes down upon her.

Yet Dearg's power was not in strength alone. Even from the rubble of wood and page, she sent forth the horde of invisible creatures she had summoned. Yet Rua could see them in the mirror, for she chose this room to fight in for this purpose. As the first shadowy figure came upon her in the glass, she knocked it aside. And then another. Then the black horse charged, and she moved like lightning out of its path, using the knife-like nails of her first two fingers to slice into its torso as it passed. In the mirror, it bucked and stumbled, and seemed to cry out. In the hall, nothing could be seen, and nothing heard.

"Magic," Rua said with scorn.

Dearg clambered up, brushing her hair aside with the back of her hand.

"You always hated it, didn't you?" Dearg challenged her.

"I always hated you."

"Well, we've been playing happy families long enough."

"Too long, it seems."

"We can end it here."

"Put your wand aside and I'll end it now."

Dearg rose, looking as haggard as ever. "I don't need a wand!" she cried, pressing both hands forward, from which shot a bolt of lightning. Rua ducked, and the bolt struck the door behind her, flinging it open. Dearg fired another, and this one bounced off the frame of the door, then off a bookcase, then to a grand piano, before striking the mirror. The glass cracked, and the reflections in it weakened. Rua stepped back towards the throne room behind her.

"You don't deserve that crown," Dearg barked, sending forth a mighty gale, which knocked the gem-encrusted tiara from Rua's head. It struck the ground with a clang, circling in place for a moment until it stood still.

"You don't deserve that life," Rua replied.

Dearg cast the winds again, forcing Rua back. It took all of the vampire queen's strength to stop from toppling over. Her scarlet dress flapped like a flag.

Once more the gale came, pushing Rua further into the throne room. Dearg advanced, picking up the crown as she passed, placing it on her own head. Yet no matter its glimmer, it did not make her look like a queen.

"The Kavanagh name ends with you," Dearg taunted.

The winds continued to propel Rua back, until she fell backwards at the foot of her own throne. To die there would have been the cruellest of fates, but by now she knew well that the fates were cruel.

Dearg raised her hands for a final assault. "Any last words?"

Rua seemed broken. The end was near. But not for her. "Yes," she said, grasping the Sceptre of the Serpent that stood resting by the arm of her throne. She pointed it towards Dearg and cried, "*Victoria Aut Mors! Vivat Regina!*"

The stone serpent that was wrapped around the sceptre suddenly came to life, darting forth towards Dearg, growing in size as it moved with a haste unknown to any of its mortal kin. Dearg tried to fire upon it, but it slithered out of the way, until finally it reached her, wrapping around her legs, and then her torso, pinning her arms down to her side so that she could make no more effort to defend herself.

Rua sauntered over, still clutching the sceptre that was now more than just a symbol of her royalty. Dearg's eyes widened as the serpent continued to squeeze. Rua drew up close to Dearg, and said, "Any final words?" Dearg opened her mouth to speak, but the serpent made its final crush, and she turned to a hail of ash. As the dust fell, Rua caught the tumbling crown. "Didn't think so."

BATS AND NAILS

The battle continued outside, vampire against vampire, but even as their numbers lessened, a new force came suddenly to join the fray: the Order of Nails. A convoy of wagons rolled in, circling the horde of the night.

The vehicles creaked into place, twenty-four in number—not because there were enough Strigoi Stalkers to fill that many, but because twenty-four was to them a holy number. Two of the wagons just housed the Torture Cubes. Another one was empty, waiting to house some more.

Lorcan had spent much of the battle diving onto unsuspecting foes, before soaring again in a flutter of black wings. He stood now on a balcony, watching as the Stalkers stabbed at every vampire clan that fought tooth and nail in the fields. The clans suddenly united against this new foe, dragging the humans to the ground, tearing off their holy armour, and tearing off their flesh as well.

Lorcan surveyed the fight, seeming unmoved by it. And then Manus drew into view, and there was a silent challenge in his stare.

Lorcan crawled out, and down the side of the building, the fabric of his gown flailing about him. The wind kept the silk billowing even as he stood still now, even as the two of them stood face-to-face in this self-made arena amidst the howling and hammering of the battle all around.

Manus swung his nail-encrusted flail, rotating it in the air, creating a whoosh of wind.

"Your time has come," he said.

"Good," Lorcan replied, hunching his shoulders. "I've had too much of it. But you, you won't have much more of it now either."

He darted forward, and Manus swung. They clashed, snarling and sneering. The flail struck flesh, but Lorcan's fingernails and fangs struck the metal of the Stalker's armour. It was strong, reinforced more by the holy symbols than by the iron, but even then it started to buckle under Lorcan's unrelenting assault.

The vampire pushed Manus back, forcing him to retreat. Again he came at him, thrashing, barely giving him a second to raise or swing the flail again. The holy symbols were no deterrent. Instead, they simply seemed to enrage Lorcan even more, making him faster, giving him strength.

Manus fell to the ground, and Lorcan leapt towards him, but just as he did, a row of Stalkers unleashed a hail of nails from their crossbows in his direction. Lorcan twisted into a cloud of bats, spreading out in all directions to avoid the barrage, before appearing again in solid form further away on the battlefield.

"Fight me like a man!" Lorcan shouted over.

Manus rose to his feet. "I can't say the same to you, demon!"

Lorcan stepped forward. A Stalker raced towards him, but he whacked the man away. And then another, who faced a similar fate. A third was much more unlucky, for Lorcan circled around him with a speed that defied sight, tearing the helmet from him, and almost his head, before sinking his teeth in deep. He didn't flick that one away. He let him slump to the ground.

Then, just as he approached Manus, three spotlights turned on from some of the wagons, shining a dazzling light at Lorcan, almost as bright and burning as the sun. He recoiled, shielding his eyes. There was a sizzle of smoke around him, and he bared his teeth, clenching them as the light seared his blanched flesh.

Manus swung his flail again, and this time it struck home more forcefully. Just as the light weakened the vampire, it strengthened the vampire-killer. Lorcan stumbled from the strike, getting back up just in time for the second swing, which knocked him down again.

Then more Stalkers came, rushing in to stab, or to lash his wrists with cuffs and chains. He cast some away, and roared at others. Then, when he rose, they yanked the chains and pulled him to the ground. Even there he fought them, raising his shackled arms, forcing them to dig their feet into the earth, and pulling them towards them, until there were none left to hold the chains. He laughed, then stopped, hunched over, to cast an evil glare at Manus.

"This is the end for you," Manus shouted.

"Don't make promises," Lorcan replied.

"It's an oath."

Lorcan smiled. "Then keep it."

Another ring of Stalkers came in, stopping any means of escape for Lorcan. He rose his hands, not in surrender, but to use his telekinetic ability to lift the ends of the chains into the air. Then he spun around, and the upraised chains struck the Stalkers standing nearby. He was like a hurricane.

He stopped, and the chains fell to the ground, though they still cuffed his wrists. He raised one arm now, letting the chain clang.

"You think this can hold me?"

With a flicker of darkness, he changed into his bat form, and the cuffs fell too. Just as quickly, he spun with a flail of his gown into his "human" form again.

"No," Manus said. "I never thought that would hold you. But I have something that will."

Lorcan knew about the Torture Cubes. He had been warned about them, and in the past he had led a raid against one of the Order of Nails' secret strongholds to free some of his fellow vampires from those awful prisons.

The Cube-holder came out behind Manus, holding up the taunting box. Lorcan felt a sudden attraction to it, but he knew that was what sucked the demon into its confines. He resisted, turning his attention back to Manus.

"There is no worse prison than this eternal life,"

he said.

"Then let me free you," Manus replied.

"You'll have to fight me."

So they fought again, the flail swinging, the nails slashing. They danced that deadly dance of circles and spirals, tearing lumps out of each other, until both were weak and wounded, until both saw vultures up above, though some were spectral ones.

But Manus was not alone. The bolts of nails came again, striking Lorcan, and the lights flared up once more. The Stalkers came in force and held him down. He writhed in place, but the holds were strong.

Manus hobbled over and knelt upon his chest. Lorcan smiled and snarled. Then Manus took that fabled nail from his belt, followed by the faithful hammer. He lined them up at Lorcan's forehead.

"Through this we cleanse even Hell itself," Manus said, repeating that sacred line.

Lorcan's smile, now less of a sneer, put Manus off. It seemed almost genuine.

"Please," he said. "End it. End it now."

Manus thought it was some trick, some attempt to delay or deceive, but there was an earnestness in Lorcan's voice, a hint of the human beneath the vampire. This one was unlike many of the others. The demon was there, but there was also something else.

"Hurry," Lorcan pleaded. "For your sake as well as mine."

Manus drove the hammer down, and the nail entered Lorcan's skull. The vampire wailed and struggled, and that same black shadow arose, drawn towards the nearby Torture Cube. Yet even as the demon was imprisoned, Lorcan spoke his dying words.

"Sweet ... release."

He turned to ash, joining the mountains of it that already littered the battlefield.

AMIDST THE RUINS

The battle was waning, and the surviving forces limped away, few in number. Rua emerged from the castle, holding up her clutched fist. Those still fighting stopped once they saw her. From that hand, she let a stream of dust fall.

"Dearg had some final words for you," she shouted. "Well, more like a final scream."

James came out to join her, brandishing the Cross of St. Benedict, which glowed much more powerfully than before. He held it aloft, and the sky seemed to brighten. The straggle of wounded vampires backed away.

"Come down to meet your death, fiends," Manus cried up to them. He was gravely maimed, and knew that he would bleed out soon. He would not survive the night, but much of the night would not survive either.

"I've met mine already," Rua said.

James shrugged. "Eh, I can wait."

"What's that?" Manus asked, staring at the cross. "Is that a blood warden in our midst?"

James stood tall. "You're damn right."

"Not damned at all then," the Stalker replied, though it was a struggle for him to talk. His fellow fighters caught him as he stumbled. "I can rest easy."

The Order of Nails retreated, taking their fallen leader with them, and also several dozen Torture Cubes, packed tight. Those who were dust on the grasses got off lightly.

Boxer from the Favoured Fangs swaggered out of the castle and wrapped his arms around Rua and James, pulling them close. "Well, it's been fun," he said. "Give us a shout the next war you're fightin'. And try not to have so much good china." He took a broken shard out of his pocket and flicked it into the air. "That's temptin', that."

Any surviving members of his gang followed him out. Neither Rua nor James had the strength to stop them, nor the will to fight. There had been too much death dealt at Umbra Montis already.

"So this is how it ends," Rua said, looking around.

James caught her gaze. "Or how it begins."

THE BLOOD CULL

The fall of the Kavanagh clan had led to many unwritten rules being broken, including the so-called "blood quota" that kept the vampire numbers down. The O'Neills were not alone in turning new vampires; other families did it too, some in open, others in secret, fearful that they would be caught without an army in the impending war. The result was over a thousand new vampires operating in Dublin alone, with many more throughout the country.

James set out on a mission to cull these numbers, to restore the balance. He was not alone in this, for the government's secretive Project Dandelion agency, and the Order of Nails, set out on their own hunting sprees. Yet it was James who proved most successful, for his power inspired a legend to unfold, which spread as fast as the plague of vampires did. It spoke of some key moments, witnessed by a few, and told to all.

Those moments happened when James rescued some tourists in the Temple Bar area from a gang of newly-turned vampires. These fiends were weak, but stronger than humans, and very thirsty. James leapt down from the roof of a nearby pub, holding aloft the Cross of St. Benedict.

"A brave one," the lead vampire said. He snarled.

"A healthy one," another added, licking her lips.

James had not left much of a mark on the lower echelons of occult society yet, but he was about to. These vampires were too fresh to have heard of him, too full of the ideals of eternal life. They hadn't yet heard of eternal death.

One of the vampires raced towards James, claws at the ready. His speed would have made the normal eyes of a human question what they had just seen, but James saw it all. He held out the cross before him like a shield, then pulled it back and punched forward.

The vampire halted, his face ashen, his mouth agape. He trembled and looked down, where he saw the shape of the cross cut straight through him. From where James was standing, he could see the figures of the other vampires through the hole.

The vampire turned to dust mid-collapse, and the others fled in all directions, climbing up buildings, running down streets. Yet before the lead vampire could escape, James fired the cross at him. As it cascaded across, the end of it sharpened, and it pierced the back of the creature, tearing into its heart and turning it to dust even as it continued to run, then stumble, away.

The cross struck the ground with a clang, rocking back and forth until it settled. It was far away now, far enough for another vampire, stalking across the rooftops, to notice. It launched itself down, ready to strike. Then something happened that James did not expect. He held his hand out for the cross, as if it was within reach, and suddenly it rose into the air and came back like a boomerang into his grasp. The assaulting vampire froze just a second before James dusted it as well.

Then James looked at his arm, and he saw a ghostly arm melding with it. He felt a presence, strong and powerful, and knew that it was Lorcan. How, he could not say, and it seemed that Lorcan had no spectral voice with which to speak. He simply extended his arm for James, using his telekinetic powers to return the cross to him.

So it was on future occasions, as James continued the cull. He launched the cross, and it came back. He held it aloft, and the weaker, fresher vampires were rent asunder by it. He made a slashing motion a metre away from them, and they were sliced in half. He made a stabbing motion just out of reach, and it was as if they had been staked by hand. None of this worked on the stronger vampires of the Five Families, who were much more resilient, but it made James a legend among the occult world, someone to be respected, and someone to be feared.

THE BOARD RESET

When the next Red Council was called, the surviving members of all Five Families were present. The O'Connors didn't have quite so many banners, and the O'Neills didn't have quite so many kin.

Rua sat upon her throne, as regal as ever, clutching her sceptre, letting the faint light shine upon her crown.

At her side sat James. He held her hand like Lorcan did, and through it, it seemed that Lorcan held it too.

"This is against tradition," Ioana Danesti said. Her family stood in disgust around her, arms folded, faces dour.

"We'll make a new tradition," Rua replied.

James smiled. "Our new perfect marriage."

"The vampire world will never accept this. They'll fight you."

James flicked the fingers of his left hand at the cross perched at his side. "I've never been more ready for a fight."

THE END

About the Author

Dean F. Wilson was born in Dublin, Ireland in 1987. He started writing at age 11, and has since become a *USA Today* and *Wall Street Journal* Bestselling Author.

He is the author of the *Children of Telm* epic fantasy trilogy, the *Great Iron War* steampunk series, the *Coilhunter Chronicles* science-fiction western series, the *Hibernian Hollows* urban fantasy series, and the *Infinite Stars* space opera series.

Dean previously worked as a journalist, primarily in the field of technology. He has written for *TechEye*, *Thinq*, *V3*, *VR-Zone*, *ITProPortal*, *TechRadar Pro*, and *The Inquirer*.

www.deanfwilson.com